HARRIET
SPIES AGAIN

Other books featuring Harriet the Spy:

Harriet the Spy

The Long Secret

Sport

HARRIET
SPIES AGAIN

Helen Ericson

DELACORTE PRESS

Published by Delacorte Press
an imprint of
Random House Children's Books
a division of Random House, Inc.
1540 Broadway
New York, New York 10036

Visit us on the Web! www.randomhouse.com/kids
Educators and librarians, for a variety of teaching tools, visit us at
www.randomhouse.com/teachers

Cataloging-in-Publication data is available from the Library of Congress.
ISBN 0-385-32786-2 (trade)—ISBN 0-385-90022-8 (lib. bdg.)

The text of this book is set in 12.5-point Goudy.
Book design by Liney Li
Manufactured in the United States of America
March 2002
10 9 8 7 6 5 4 3 2 1
BVG

HARRIET
SPIES AGAIN

CHAPTER 1

"I won't go," Harriet told her parents. She glared at them.

Her parents had called her down from her room while she was busy on a project. Ordinarily the cook served Harriet her dinner at six in the kitchen while her parents had martinis in the living room. Harriet looked at her watch. It was exactly six. So not only had they interrupted her project, but now they were making her late for her dinner, which was very likely getting cold.

She had been making a time line of her life. By taping sheets of paper carefully together, she had created a strip so long it reached from the door of her bedroom to the bottom of the old toy box that held all her notebooks. It had taken her twelve pieces of paper. Since Harriet would be twelve on her next birthday, she had designated one sheet for each year of her life. Then she had begun to fill in the important events. But she had barely finished half of the first page when her mother interrupted her.

SIX MONTHS. SPEAKS FIRST WORD, Harriet had just written halfway across the first-year page. She thought for a moment about what her first word might have been. She pictured herself at six months old, with her nursemaid poised over the bassinet looking down at her, probably holding a warm milk–filled bottle. What might she have said?

FIRST WORD she wrote as a subcategory. She thought about it for a while, trying to decide what a first word might be, at least a first word from the lips of a highly intelligent New York infant named Harriet M. Welsch. Carefully she printed PROCEED.

Then she went on to SEVEN MONTHS. SPEAKS FIRST SENTENCE. FIRST SENTENCE: PROCEED WITH THE FEEDING, PLEASE.

"Harriet, dear?" her mother had called up the stairs to Harriet's cozy bedroom at the top of the tall, narrow house. "Would you come down, please?"

Reluctantly Harriet had rolled up her time line and headed down the two long flights of stairs to the double living room on the first floor. "I hope we didn't interrupt anything important, dear," Mrs. Welsch said after Harriet entered the living room and sat down on a dark red velvet chair. Harriet shrugged. They would not understand the time line. It would make them feel nervous and uncertain, she thought. Her parents frequently felt nervous and uncertain about her projects.

So she said only, "I was just thinking about my infancy. Do you happen to remember my first word?"

"Of course I do! Parents never forget such things," Mrs. Welsch said. She turned to her husband. "Harry, tell Harriet what her first word was!"

Harriet's father stared blankly at her.

Mrs. Welsch gave a thin laugh. "It was *cookie*, dear. You were about fourteen months old, and one day you quite clearly said *cookie*."

"And my first sentence?" Harriet asked, glumly realizing that she would have to start her time line over with the correct information. Cross-outs were unacceptable and Harriet only used pens. Just last Christmas her parents had given her a wonderful dark green Waterman pen, which she treasured and used as often as possible. "What was my first sentence?"

"Well, you combined a verb and a noun, dear. You said, 'Gimme cookie.' "

"Oh," Harriet said. Well, she thought, I won't bother to erase after all. It's essentially the same thing as "Proceed with the feeding."

"Why did you want me to come down?" she asked her parents.

"We have some news to share with you. Would you like a peanut, by the way?" Mrs. Welsch put her martini down and passed a small silver dish of peanuts to Harriet.

Harriet shook her head. Ordinarily she liked peanuts, but for some reason she could feel her appetite disappearing. It made her uncomfortable when her parents announced news. Their news never seemed to be the kind of news Harriet wanted to hear. "What news?" she asked.

"Your father has received a rather important assignment from the network. Harry, wouldn't you like to describe it to Harriet?"

Mr. Welsch had been looking at the folded newspaper on the table near the peanut dish. He was pretending not to. But Harriet could see him surreptitiously glancing at the day's headlines. "Paris," he said.

"Paris?" asked Harriet with suspicion. "France?"

"We're to leave next week for Paris!" Mrs. Welsch explained in the same perky, delighted voice that she used to describe bridge tournaments or antiques auctions.

"For how long?" Harriet wasn't deceived by the voice. A little vacation in Paris would be okay, she thought. Maybe it would be a pleasant interlude before school resumed next month. But she had an ominous feeling. She was glad she hadn't accepted a peanut. It might have lulled her too quickly into a cheerful reaction, when really *suspicion* was called for.

Her mother wiped her lips tidily, using a small cocktail napkin printed with a red-and-green design of olives in a stack. She said something that sounded like *twamah* while holding the napkin in front of her mouth.

"*Twamah?*" Harriet repeated, wondering if perhaps her mother was speaking French, although Harriet had studied French for two years already, in fifth and sixth grades, and *twamah* had not been a vocabulary word.

"*Trois mois,*" Mr. Welsch said quite clearly and with an air of impatience. "We're going to live in Paris for three months, beginning next week."

"The network has rented a lovely apartment for us, dear," Mrs. Welsch said. "Quite near the Luxembourg Gardens. *Les jardins,* I mean."

In her mind Harriet leapt ahead on her time line to the final sheet, the one for her twelfth year, the one that she wedged under a corner of her old toy box when the long strip was unrolled on the floor of her room. AGE ALMOST-TWELVE: MOVES TO PARIS. It was not what she had had in mind for age almost-twelve.

"I won't go," she told her parents, glaring. Then she added, "And in case you missed it, I expostulated that."

Her father looked at her through his glasses. Harriet's father was a television executive. He had an executive face, and hair that was combed in an executive way.

"Excuse me?" Mr. Welsch said.

Harriet imagined how he must look in his office when some poor scriptwriter, nervous and hungry, sat before him with a manuscript held together by a frayed rubber band and pleaded for a chance to be head writer on a sitcom so he could pay his debts and feed his starving children. Her father would probably look down through his glasses the same way. He would probably say in that same executive voice, "Excuse me?"

Harriet sighed. She repeated it. "I won't go," she said for the second time.

"No, no, I understood that part," her father said. He sipped his martini. "I didn't understand what you added, about expostulating."

"Oh. Well," Harriet explained, "Mr. Grenville says—"

Harriet's mother interrupted. "Mr. Grenville is one of Harriet's teachers at school, dear," she told Harriet's father.

He nodded. Harriet could tell he was making a note of that in his head. "Go on," he said.

"Mr. Grenville says we must use strong verbs when we write."

"Strong verbs?" Mr. Welsch took another sip of his drink.

"Yes. For example, instead of just saying 'He walked,' we should say 'He ambled.' Or 'He strolled.' "

"I see."

"And instead of 'She said,' it would be better to use a strong verb."

"Like *expostulate*, perhaps?" Harriet's father asked.

"Exactly. *Expostulate* is my current favorite. I have a list of favorite strong verbs in my notebook."

"And so when you told us that you wouldn't go, you wanted to be certain that we understood you weren't simply *saying* it. You were—"

"Expostulating," Harriet said.

"I see."

"She's very clever, dear, isn't she?" Mrs. Welsch said to her husband. She looked proudly at Harriet, who was sitting stiffly on the dark red velvet chair still glaring at both of her parents. Then she held the small dish of peanuts toward Harriet again, but Harriet once more declined. She was hoping that her failure to take a peanut—combined with the expostulating—would indicate to them how outraged she was.

"It is outrageous," she said. "The whole idea is outrageous." Harriet liked the sound of that. Probably, she decided, she would add *outrageous* to the list of strong adjectives she was also keeping in her notebook. "And I absolutely will not go."

"Harriet," said her father, and now he finished the last drops of his martini, set the glass down, and reached for the newspaper, "we were not planning to take you."

. . .

As she had feared, her dinner was cold. Cook had not even had the courtesy to keep it warm in the oven for her. Harriet sat down at the round wooden table in the kitchen, unfolded her napkin, and frowned at her plate. Chicken. Chicken was okay cold. Salad. That was *supposed* to be cold, so Harriet couldn't complain about the salad, though she turned the lettuce leaves over carefully with her fork to make certain there were no lurking onions. Cook knew that Harriet loathed raw onions but sometimes she sneaked them in anyway. Not tonight. No onions, Harriet noted with relief.

But there were mashed potatoes on the plate. Few things in the world were worse than cold mashed potatoes. They tainted the other food, Harriet decided after a moment. So she stood up, carried her plate to the sink, and noisily scraped the potatoes into the garbage. Cook watched her.

"Wouldn't be cold if you'd come on time," Cook said pointedly.

Harriet sat back down at the table and stabbed a bit of chicken with her fork. She vaguely wanted to say something disagreeable and sharp-tongued to Cook. It was their usual mode of communication, although they were surprisingly fond of each other. But no words came to her. She poked at the chicken again and realized to her horror that she was starting to cry.

Crying! And she would be twelve years old in October!

Cook hadn't noticed yet. "You're pretty quiet tonight for someone whose mouth usually goes yammer yammer yammer," she said, leaning over the stove to stir whatever she was preparing for Harriet's parents' dinner.

Harriet gave an enormous sniff and tried very hard to make it sound like a sarcastic one, but it didn't. It was quite wet, actually more a snuffle than a sniff, and she had to grab her napkin and hold it to her face.

"I got a bad feeling," Cook said, "it's not mashed potatoes making you that miserable."

"No," Harriet wailed. "They're going to Paris and they're not taking me!" Even as she wailed it, Harriet remembered that she didn't *want* to live in Paris. She wanted to live right here in New York, in this tall, skinny house on East Eighty-seventh Street where she had lived all her life, nearly twelve years so far.

"Oh, that," said Cook.

Harriet finished one final sniff, wiped her nose on her napkin, and looked at Cook suspiciously. "What do you mean 'Oh, that?' Did you know already?"

Cook nodded. "Yeah, they're paying me to stay on and cook. Wanted to pay me *less* because there won't be so much cooking with them gone. But then they found out that those people across the street . . ." She gestured toward the small window that looked out onto the sidewalk. Because the kitchen was in the basement, Harriet and Cook could watch people's feet through the window, and they often did. Feet were interesting, Harriet thought. She had been thinking about adding foot and shoe observations to her notes on her spy route.

Now Harriet looked through the window because Cook was pointing in that direction. She saw a pair of high-heeled brown leather boots walk past, followed by a small fuzzy dog on a leash. Suddenly the dog stopped, sniffed the small wrought-iron fence that enclosed the kitchen window, and raised his leg alongside it. Harriet looked away to give the dog the privacy she felt he deserved.

Cook wasn't referring to the passing pedestrians, anyway. She meant, Harriet knew, the people who lived directly across the street in a brownstone house almost identical to the Welsches'. Their name was Feigenbaum. Dr. Feigenbaum was a psychiatrist and had an office on the first floor of their house. His wife, who had an office upstairs, was a doctor who specialized in women, which Harriet thought was a very limited specialty; Harriet preferred uni-sex everything, especially clothes. Somewhere in the midst of all those offices the two Dr. Fei-genbaums also lived. Harriet, who had been a spy since she was eight, had been spying on the Fei-genbaums for several years. She felt that they had some deeply hidden secrets and a life lacking in emotional depth.

They also were lacking in competent domestic help, Harriet knew, and frequently tried to hire Cook away from the Welsches.

"They tried again?" Harriet asked.

"Yeah, offered me full time, full pay. Seemed like a good time to make the move, with your parents away and all. You going to eat that or not?" Cook began to pick up Harriet's plate. Harriet looked at her uneaten chicken, suddenly decided she was hungry after all, and snatched the plate back. "I'm eating it," she said. "Don't get grabby."

Cook pulled out one of the other chairs that matched the pine table and sat down. Harriet could tell Cook wanted a cigarette. Harriet knew that sometimes she went out into the back courtyard and smoked.

"I might consider letting you smoke in the kitchen when they're gone," Harriet said slyly. "The Feigenbaums never would. They'd give you pamphlets about lung cancer." She stacked three cucumber slices on top of one another and speared them with her fork.

Cook sighed. "I already said I was staying. Your parents talked me into it. They're paying me my full salary. We're still arguing about weekends, though."

Weekends. Hearing the word gave Harriet an odd sensation in her stomach. Cook always left on Friday night after dinner and usually didn't return until Sunday night. Harriet ordinarily spent her weekends spying, reading, and spending time with her best friends, Simon Rocque, aka Sport, and Janie Gibbs, who both lived nearby. She supposed she would still do that. But if Cook left on Friday night, the house would be empty. Harriet didn't really like the idea of coming home to an empty house. Of *sleeping* in an empty house.

"I'm not sure it's legal, actually, to leave an eleven-year-old alone for a whole weekend," Harriet said. "For three months of weekends. *Twamah* of weekends. Of course, I'm quite competent. More competent than the *usual* eleven-year-old. But the Department of Child Welfare may look on it somewhat differently, and I suspect—"

"Yammer yammer yammer," said Cook, and she got up and went to the stove to stir things again.

"And I hope you don't think I'm going with you to Brooklyn on weekends," Harriet went on. "I like your house just fine, Cook, and I like your sister, and I enjoy going to your church. But I do not like your son one bit. He's very sarcastic, and I think he has a personality disorder. And anyway, I have things to do on weekends. I'm behind in my spying."

"Yammer," Cook said. "What makes you think I want you in my house in Brooklyn every weekend? I have things to do, too, and they don't include you, Harriet Welsch."

Harriet picked up her empty plate and took it to the sink. "So you'll just go off and leave me here alone?" she asked. "I'm nonplussed by that." Nonplussed, Harriet said again to herself, liking the sound of it, and deciding to try to use it more often.

"Who said you'll be alone?"

"But if you go to Brooklyn—"

"You mean they didn't tell you?"

"Tell me *what?*" Harriet remembered suddenly that she had stomped out of the living room while her parents were still talking about the plans they had made. Maybe she should have stayed and listened.

"Miss Golly's coming back." Cook rinsed Harriet's plate and loaded it into the dishwasher. "That uppity old thing." She began to gather silverware to set the table for Harriet's parents' dinner.

"*Ole Golly?* She's coming back?"

"Didn't I just say that? You deaf?"

Harriet threw her arms around the cook. "Oh!" she cried. "Cooky, Cooky, Cooky, I love you so much! No wonder you were my very first word! No wonder I said 'Gimme cookie'!" In exhilaration she kissed Cook on her astonished mouth.

Upstairs, the clock in the front hall bonged suddenly. Seven bongs. With a scowl Cook pried Harriet loose and lifted her apron to wipe the kiss away. "Quit that nonsense," she said. "Now go tell your parents that their dinner will be on the table in five minutes, and that the reason it's late is because you wouldn't eat and you blubbered and yammered, so they better not blame me." Briskly she carried place mats and silver to the table in the adjoining dining room.

Harriet sped up the stairs. Ole Golly's coming back! Ole Golly's coming back! she sang to herself as she emerged on the first floor. The living room was empty. "I'm nonplussed!" she sang aloud as she sped up the next flight and started on the third, toward her bedroom. "Nonplussed!"

Then she remembered her parents and turned back. They were in the library on the second floor. Her father was still reading the newspaper he had begun in the living room, and her mother was laying out a game of solitaire on the small mahogany table between the front windows.

"Your dinner is just about to be served!" Harriet sang in a soprano voice, pretending to be a singer on the stage of the Metropolitan Opera. Then she curtseyed and blew kisses to her parents, who were both staring at her in a nonplussed way, and continued up the final flight of stairs to her room, where she flung herself onto her bed and lay smiling at the ceiling, overwhelmed with happiness.

CHAPTER 2

Sometimes Harriet wondered what it would be like to have siblings. When she was younger, about nine, she had devoted several pages in her notebook to speculation on that topic.

IF I HAD A SISTER WE COULD TALK AT NIGHT AFTER WE WERE IN BED. WE COULD DISCUSS OUR PARENTS BEHIND THEIR BACKS, WHETHER THEIR MARRIAGE WAS A SATISFY-ING ONE, AND IF NOT, HOW THEY COULD IMPROVE IT, AND ALSO WHAT THEY MIGHT BE GIVING US FOR CHRISTMAS AND WHERE IT MIGHT BE HIDDEN.

But it was clear that a sister was not ever going to materialize in her life, or a brother, either, except for the Christian Children's Fund child in an orphanage in Cambodia, whose photograph was thumbtacked to the bulletin board in the kitchen. Harriet was glad her parents sent him money so he could have schoolbooks, but she didn't think he qualified at all as a brother even though her parents tried to pass him off on her that way. And she wished the orphanage where he lived had a unisex beauty parlor because he had a very rectangular-looking haircut and it was quite unflattering.

Without siblings, Harriet relied heavily on the telephone for communication. She felt very fortunate to have a phone in the hall outside her bedroom. It had been installed there for Ole Golly years before so she could call an ambulance if baby Harriet had an attack of appendicitis or poison ivy in the middle of the night. But the telephone had a very long, curled-up cord. So Harriet could stretch it into her room to talk to her friends Sport and Janie in privacy. And Ole Golly, when she had still lived in the yellow bedroom across the hall, could stretch it into *her* bedroom and talk to her mother, Mrs. Golly, who lived in Far Rockaway. Later, after Ole Golly had met George Waldenstein and added romance to her life last year, Harriet supposed she had stretched the cord and talked to him, too, late at night.

Though her spying abilities had become quite sophisticated by then, Harriet had never spied or eavesdropped on Ole Golly and Mr. Waldenstein during their courtship, except for one time when she had been curious about kissing. If she had paid more attention, had spied more industriously, she might not have been quite so surprised when they announced their engagement.

Harriet was glad that no one had thought to remove the third-floor telephone after Ole Golly had become Mrs. Waldenstein and moved to Montreal. Often in the evening Harriet talked to her friends. Tonight she called Sport.

"Sport? Are you busy?"

"What do you mean?" he asked. "Of *course* I'm busy. I made lasagna for dinner. It takes forever to get a lasagna casserole clean. I'm soaking it for the second time."

Harriet sighed. Sport's father, Matthew Rocque, was a writer. He was very good at writing but hopeless at any domestic task, so Sport had been in charge of cooking and cleaning and even the household budget for several years. Once Harriet had thought about asking Cook to prepare extra meals that they could freeze and deliver once a week to Sport's apartment, sort of a Meals on Wheels for the not particularly elderly. Then she had remembered that the apartment was on the fourth floor, with no elevator. And she remembered, too, that Sport took a certain pride in his cooking.

Quite recently Sport had acquired a stepmother. But apparently he wasn't ready to give up control of his household.

"Why doesn't Kate cook, Sport?" Harriet asked.

"She will, sometimes. We're still working out the details of that. There will be a lot of compromises," Sport explained. "But for now, I'm still in charge of the meals."

"I do not understand one bit why people get married," Harriet said.

"Love," Sport replied, as if the answer were obvious.

"But—" Harriet began, and then stopped. Sport was not the person to answer her questions about love. And she knew she'd never want to discuss it with her parents. She decided she would ask Ole Golly, who of course would be an expert, having just gotten married a few months before.

"Well, I wanted to tell you that I have a lot of

plans for tomorrow." Harriet took a piece of paper from her pocket and looked at the list she'd been making.

"Me too. I'll still be working on this casserole. The cheese got all burned on one side. I think I'll probably soak it in a mixture of ammonia and water overnight."

"Ammonia and water? Isn't that dangerous?"

"No, not unless you mix chlorine in. Then it releases a deadly poison gas."

"Oh." Harriet scrunched her nose thinking about it.

"I'll wear rubber gloves, though, when I do it. My hands are getting all cruddy from detergent."

Harriet wondered briefly, as she had many times before, what life would be like for Sport in seventh grade. The Gregory School, which they had attended together for so many years, didn't allow boys beyond the sixth grade. So Sport would be starting next month at a different school, and Harriet was very much afraid that the students there would not understand Sport's commitment to housework and cooking and that they might make fun.

"What time are you going to be finished in the morning?" she asked him. Then she waited, knowing from the silence that he was calculating.

Finally he replied. "Ten twenty-five," he said, "unless anything unusual happens."

Again Harriet worried briefly. The students at his new school would have a very hard time understanding Sport, she knew.

"I'll call you then, okay?" Harriet told Sport. "I plan to spy on the Feigenbaums tomorrow. Want to come?"

"I might. Depends."

Harriet looked at her list. PREPARE YELLOW BEDROOM. "In the afternoon," she said, "I'll be doing some domestic stuff. You might want to help. I have to fix up Ole Golly's room, because something truly monumental has happened. She's coming back!"

"Ole Golly's coming back?" Sport almost shouted into the telephone. "Out-bloody-*standing!*"

Harriet agreed. She said goodbye so Sport could get back to his soaking casserole.

• • •

"Harriet, dear?"

Harriet jumped. Her mother was at her bedroom door. Ordinarily her mother came up to the third-floor bedroom only to give her daughter a good-night kiss. But by then Harriet was always already in bed, and her things were neatly put away: her note-book inside the old toy box, her projects and charts and lists in her desk drawers. Harriet was a very organized person. Of course, spies *had* to be. It wouldn't do for a spy to lose things, or to mix them together.

But tonight her mother appeared earlier than usual, and Harriet, having taken a bath and changed into her pajamas, was sprawled on the floor working on her time line. It was unrolled, stretched across the rug. At least, Harriet thought gratefully, she hadn't yet tacked it to the wall. She intended to do that eventually, and she was fairly certain her mother would not be thrilled.

"My goodness!" Mrs. Welsch said when she entered the room. "Harriet, you are such a busy little bee! Whatever are you working on now?"

Harriet sighed and wondered whether she could hunch her body over in a way that would conceal the time line. But her body was only a little more than five feet long, and her time line was considerably longer than that. Her time line was about the same length as a lying-down professional basketball player. There was no way to conceal it.

So she did the next best thing. She lifted the

corner of the toy box where it weighted one end of her work. The paper popped loose, and Harriet watched as the time line magically curled itself up.

"I'm studying how springs work," Harriet told her mother pleasantly. It was a lie. Spies often lied.

"Aren't you clever, darling! Have you thought about examining your bedspring?" Mrs. Welsch crossed the room, lifted the edge of the blue bedspread, and examined the construction of Harriet's bed. She looked puzzled for a moment. Then she said, "Oh. It's not visible. Well, that's why they're called *inner*springs, I guess."

Harriet replaced the rubber band around her time line and put it in her desk drawer. She went to her bed, pulled the blue spread all the way down, and climbed in. "By the way, I don't mind that you're going to Paris," she told her mother.

"We'll be back in November, dear," her mother said, smoothing Harriet's hair. "And won't it be lovely for you, having Miss Golly back? I know you've missed her."

"She probably wishes we could go to Paris with you."

Mrs. Welsch looked startled at the thought. "My goodness," she said. "That never occurred to us, dear."

"I don't want to go to Paris. I can't pronounce most of the words, even the so-called easy ones. Like *oeuf* or *oeil*. Who makes words with three vowels in a row? It should be illegal."

Her mother smiled. "A lot of things are different in France," she said. "They even let dogs into restaurants. Imagine! I'm not sure I'll like that. I wonder if they have a no-dogs section."

"Well, Ole Golly wouldn't like a restaurant with dogs in it, I can tell you that! She would probably speak very, very harshly to the waiter," Harriet said. "But she did say that she would like to travel.

"I think that's partly why she married Mr. Waldenstein," Harriet confided. "So that she could go to Montreal."

"Harriet, dear?"

"Does Mr. Waldenstein mind that she's coming back to New York? Daddy would mind if you went to live someplace else, I think."

"Harriet, dear? Listen to me a minute."

"What?"

Mrs. Welsch bit her lip. "How shall I say this? Things haven't worked out well for Miss Golly, dear, in Montreal. And I have, ah, promised her that we will never mention Mr. Waldenstein's name."

"But he's her husband! How can you not ever mention her husband?"

Mrs. Welsch sighed. "She said to me on the telephone that Mr. Waldenstein has ceased to exist. That we must expunge him from our memory, as she has."

Expunge, thought Harriet, and resolved to write it down on her list of strong verbs.

"In any case"—Mrs. Welsch was using her perky voice again—"isn't it fortunate for us that just when we *need* her, she is available! Fate at work, I would say, wouldn't you, Harriet?"

Harriet wouldn't, exactly. For one thing, now she had *no one* to ask about love. But she nodded politely. "When is she coming? I have to prepare."

"Next Tuesday morning. And our plane leaves for Paris Tuesday evening. Goodness, I must prepare, too! The packing! The shopping! I'll be very busy this weekend, Harriet. Will you be able to manage? Would you like to go to Brooklyn with Cook?"

Harriet shook her head. It was tempting. But she had so much to do to prepare for Ole Golly. Her mother had no idea.

"No," she said sleepily. "I'll stay here."

"Good night, darling," Harriet's mother said, and

kissed her cheek. "Sleep well." She turned out the light and tiptoed away.

Harriet lay silently in the dark for a moment, thinking. Then she turned the light back on, got out of bed, found the key where she kept it hidden, and opened the toy box. She still called it the toy box— still thought of it as the toy box—even though it hadn't contained toys for many years, not since Harriet had decided to become a spy. The toy box was the only container she owned that could be locked. Her spy notebooks were all inside.

Kneeling on the floor beside the toy box, Harriet took out her current notebook, a green composition notebook like all the rest. She flipped through it, looking for an empty page. FLOSS, she found on a recent one, and she remembered writing that after a lecture from her dentist, Dr. Van Pelt. She looked at that page for a moment and decided it was boring and unworthy. So she tore it out and threw it into her wastebasket.

EXPUNGE MR. WALDENSTEIN FROM MY MEMORY, she wrote carefully on a fresh page. But she knew it would be difficult.

Just there, in the corner of the toy box, was one of her first notebooks. Most of it was about Ole Golly. Although the early notes were babyish things, written in babyish penmanship—not even cursive at first, and not always spelled correctly—she felt nostalgic about them as she reread.

OLE GOLLY IS SO MEAN, SHE SAYS I HAVE TO LEARN THREE NEW WORDS EVRY DAY. CRUEL, HORRIBEL, WARLIKE, THOSE ARE MY 3 TODAY.

WHO CARES ABOUT POSCHER. I DON'T. ONLY OLE GOLLY DOES.

Harriet frowned when she read that one, trying to remember what *poscher* might be. Perhaps a kind of European oatmeal, like muesli? Then she recalled Ole Golly's voice: "Harriet, sit up straight. You never know who might be admiring you." Of course! Posture! Ole Golly had always been a stickler for good posture. She was right, too, Harriet knew now. Sport had actually told her once that he found her ramrod-like posture remarkable.

On another page, one with notes about Sport, she knew she would find the word *ramrod*. But she wouldn't bother searching for that one now. Now was the time to look back over the years with Ole Golly—and the months with Mr. Waldenstein—anticipating the return of one and expunging the memory of the other.

* * *

It had been Ole Golly, after all, who had encouraged Harriet's career as a spy. Harriet had said to her once, when they were sitting in Ole Golly's yellow bedroom across the hall on a quiet evening, that she wanted to know everything about everything. Some people might have laughed at that ambition. Some people thought an ambition should be finding a cure for cancer, or hitting the home run that wins the World Series. Harriet didn't think those were *dumb* ambitions; she just thought they were *limited*.

"I want to know everything in the world, everything," Harriet had announced suddenly. Ole Golly had been reading that evening. She was reading a book called *Dostoievsky*. It was fat enough that it probably contained everything about everything.

"I will be a spy," Harriet had said, and Ole Golly had not laughed or been nonplussed. She had put her book down for a moment and looked thoughtful. Then she had said, "It won't do you a bit of good to know everything if you don't do anything with it." So Harriet had decided not only to be a spy, not only to learn everything about everything, but also to do something with it. She felt now that she had succeeded in some ways. She had become a masterful spy—the many notebooks in her locked toy box were proof of that.

But she had not always been so masterful. Just last year her notebook had fallen into the hands of her classmates—many of whom were the very people she spied on. The results had been disastrous. But Harriet had learned a great deal from the experience. She did not yet know everything about everything, but you couldn't expect to when you were not quite twelve. That would come later, Harriet thought, and she looked forward to the moment when she would wake up one morning and realize: I know everything about everything! the way Dostoievsky must have.

As for doing anything with it, as Ole Golly had advised, Harriet was uncertain. Sometimes she did things with the information she obtained by spying, but they were smallish things. Desire was there, but opportunity was lacking. She sat on the floor with her notebook open and yearned for an opportunity to use her knowledge in a broad and important way.

A folded paper fell suddenly into Harriet's lap, right onto her lavender-striped pajamas. She picked it up, recognized it, and smiled. It was the letter that

Ole Golly had sent after she had married and moved to Montreal.

. . . If you're missing me I want you to know I'm not missing you. Gone is gone. I never miss anything or anyone because it all becomes a lovely memory. I guard my memories and love them, but I don't get in them and lie down. . . .

Harriet had memorized that part. She had memorized almost the entire letter. She had even kissed the folded letter several times, and she did so again, kissing it goodbye before replacing it between the pages of the notebook. This time there was no sadness in her kiss, because there was no farewell. Ole Golly was returning.

Climbing back into her bed after putting the notebook away, Harriet recalled the ending of the letter:

No more nonsense.
Ole Golly Waldenstein

Expunge George Waldenstein, Harriet commanded herself. In her mind she changed the signature simply to *Ole Golly*, deleting the last name as a way of expunging. It seemed a strange request— to expunge your husband. Harriet recognized when something seemed peculiar, but then Ole Golly wasn't like everybody—or anybody—else.

Harriet turned over into her sleeping position, thinking about her spying plans for the weekend, and in the back of her mind looking forward to Tuesday.

CHAPTER 3

Harriet prepared to set out shortly after breakfast on Saturday morning. She had eaten cornflakes and a banana in the kitchen.

When Cook was there, sometimes Harriet liked to place an order as if she were in a fine restaurant. "I believe I'd like a cheese omelet with fresh parsley snippered on top of it, and a little crisp bacon on the side, please," she would say. Harriet enjoyed the look on Cook's face when she placed an order.

"We're out of that," Cook would say, "and you get scrambled or nothing."

But there was no fun in playing fine restaurant on Cook's days off, so Harriet always ate cornflakes and a banana.

From her bedroom, as she gathered her spying equipment after breakfast, she could hear her mother talking on the phone downstairs in the library.

"No, she's just fine with it, Sylvia," Mrs. Welsch was saying. Harriet knew they were talking about her. Conversations that used *she* were usually about Harriet.

Sylvia was Mrs. Welsch's best friend, Sylvia Connelly, who lived in a very fancy apartment near Central Park. Harriet didn't like Sylvia Connelly very much. Sylvia didn't understand children, in Harriet's opinion, even though she had two of her own awful boys, twins named Malcolm and Edmund, who went away to a military school where they were learning more than any human should ever know about weapons and warfare. How Mr. and Mrs. Connelly were able to love Malcolm and Edmund was yet one more of the mysteries Harriet had not been able to solve.

Malcolm's and Edmund's names had been taken from Shakespeare plays, which Harriet thought was a very dumb way to choose children's names because what if someone got Hamlet or Iago? They would not have one single friend at school because everyone would just be laughing at them about their names.

Harriet had been named for her father, Harry Welsch. She had added the M. herself, since she had no middle name and felt deprived. M. didn't stand for a name. It stood for *middle*.

"Well, of course we could have taken her along and put her into a French school—what do they call them? A *lycée*? *École*? Whatever. But she has her friends here, and her projects—"

She paused for a moment, and Harriet knew that Sylvia Connelly was yammering. Yammer yammer yammer.

"You're a dear," her mother went on. "Yes, do invite her over now and then. She'd love it."

Harriet sighed and attached her pliers to her belt. She patted her back pocket to be certain her notebook was there, and her shirt pocket to check on her pen. She looked at her watch: 9:41. She listened from the top of the stairs and determined that her mother had finished talking to Sylvia and maybe the telephone would be available for a minute or two before one of them called the other again. Sport would still be busy with his lasagna pan, she knew, but she dialed his number anyway.

No answer. Harriet had expected that. Sport often didn't take calls when he was busy with housework. And his father was rarely there now that Kate had become part of his life. He and Kate were still in the romantic early-marriage stage where they did things like go to the zoo or ride the Staten Island ferry. Harriet had noticed that lovers and newlyweds in movies—at least movies set in New York—all did exactly the same things: ferry, zoo, bookstore, Chinese restaurant, and Greenwich Village. After they did all those things about forty times, always holding hands and smooching, then, Harriet supposed, real life could start.

In the meantime real people like Sport and Harriet had to hold down the fort, spying and washing lasagna dishes.

CONTINUING FEIGENBAUM INVESTIGATION
SATURDAY MORNING, AUGUST 19TH

Harriet made the note, replaced the notebook in her pocket, and headed down the stairs. As she passed her parents' bedroom, she could see open suitcases on the bed and a stack of her mother's sweaters folded on a chair. She heard her mother dialing. "Syl?" her mother said into the telephone. "I just thought of one other thing. . . ."

Yammer yammer yammer. Harriet continued

down the second flight of stairs and went out through the front door onto East Eighty-seventh Street.

*   *   *

Qualms was a word Harriet liked a lot. It was on several of her lists, and she hoped fervently that someday she would be able to use it in a Scrabble game, maybe when Ole Golly was reinstalled in her third-floor bedroom. Harriet and Ole Golly had often played Scrabble.

Now, though, returning from Montreal, where she had probably taken up speaking French because Montreal was in the French-speaking part of Canada, Ole Golly might very well be equipped with a lot of *Q* words. Harriet knew from fifth- and sixth-grade French class that the language did use *Q*s in frequent and mystifying ways, such as *Qu'est-ce que c'est?* Harriet had learned to say that pretty well, repeating it and repeating it along with the entire class, but she thought it a very strange phrase, and she still didn't understand how it went together or how the French had thought it up.

She crossed the street when the light at the corner turned red and the stream of traffic let up. She decided to make a Scrabble rule for the future: no French.

That still allowed for *qualms*, Harriet thought with satisfaction.

She had no qualms about the intrusions good spying required. She had lurked often and eavesdropped many, many times. Lurking and eavesdropping were, Harriet knew, socially unacceptable. But not for spies.

Once, she had even hidden in a dumbwaiter, all folded up and uncomfortable, to collect information about a mysterious neighbor. She did not plan to do that again.

She walked to the end of the block, around the corner, and down a narrow alley into a passageway that would take her to the backyard of the Feigenbaums' brownstone. Beside their fence, hidden by two large trash cans, Harriet knelt and made notes.

PERSON PASSES TO AND FRO IN FRONT OF KITCHEN WINDOW. CANNOT BE COOK. IF THEY HAD COOK THEY WOULD NOT KEEP TRYING TO STEAL OURS.

Harriet looked at that paragraph, loving the word *fro*. She closed her notebook and peered through the fence at the Feigenbaums' kitchen window. Then she reopened her notebook and added:

SHORT PERSON WITH PONYTAIL.

As Harriet watched, the short, ponytailed figure opened the refrigerator, stood there a moment indecisively, and then took out a bottle of what appeared to be orange juice. Then, holding the bottle, the person moved out of Harriet's range of vision.

A gray-and-white cat appeared, stretching itself flat under the fence and then popping back into its normal shape. It rubbed itself against Harriet's high-top hiking boot. She scratched its neck while she thought.

Neither Feigenbaum has a ponytail. So this is a stranger. Possibly a home invader. They could be in danger. They may be hostages.

She waited a few moments, watching for a reappearance of the stranger or a glimpse of a bound-and-gagged Feigenbaum. But nothing moved past the windows.

Harriet decided to make an appearance at the front of the house to attract the attention of the stranger. It was a dangerous move, she knew.

Therefore, she decided to rewrite her will before going any further.

Harriet had several copies of her will and always carried one with her. She sighed, took out her notebook again, and removed the folded will from between the back pages. It was a nuisance rewriting the will because each time she rewrote it, she had to remember to change all existing copies. But sometimes, especially in dangerous situations, it had to be done.

LAST WILL AND TESTAMENT OF HARRIET M. WELSCH

Harriet glanced at the pages and realized that the will was due for revision anyway because she had written Ole Golly out when she married and moved away. Hastily, kneeling behind the trash cans, she wrote Ole Golly back in.

I BEQUEATH MY TIME LINE AND MY SCRABBLE DICTIONARY TO CATHERINE GOLLY WALDENSTEIN.

She chewed on her pen for a moment and then added:

OR, AS SHE APPARENTLY PREFERS TO BE KNOWN NOW, CATHERINE GOLLY.

Quickly she reread the rest of her will, which left all her spying equipment and her notebooks to Simon Rocque, aka Sport; her clothes and tennis racket to Beth Ellen Hansen; and her last three years of science projects, all currently located in the storage area off the Welsches' kitchen, to Janie Gibbs.

ALL ELSE TO THE HOMELESS, Harriet wrote in carefully. THIS INCLUDES MY LAMP DESIGNED TO LOOK LIKE A HEINZ KETCHUP BOTTLE, WHICH I BOUGHT AT A YARD SALE WHEN I WAS SEVEN.

From time to time she worried about the future of that lamp and whether homeless people would have a place to plug it in. But she didn't know how else to bequeath her lamp, since everyone she knew, including Sport and Janie, hated it.

Finally, feeling that she had disposed of her worldly goods satisfactorily, Harriet headed to the front of the Feigenbaums' house. Boldly, without hesitation, she climbed the front steps and rang the doorbell. She had often observed the Feigenbaums' patients doing this as she watched from her own house. All of Barbara Feigenbaum's patients were female, and many of them were pregnant, some quite huge. All of Morris Feigenbaum's patients looked completely average, like businessmen, housewives, bus drivers, or convenience-store owners. Harriet supposed that beneath their average exteriors they had deeply troubled souls. Sometimes she watched through binoculars to see if their hands trembled as they rang the bell of their psychiatrist's office.

After ringing the bell, they would say something—their names, she guessed—into the little speaker. Then the door would be released and they would enter for their appointments.

"Yes?" A voice greeted her through the speaker as she stood on the steps. It sounded like a receptionist, not a home invader.

"Dr. Hrrmmmpphhhrr," Harriet muttered.

"Say again?"

"Rummmffffsshh."

The door clicked and unlocked itself. Harriet entered.

●　●　●

Interesting, Harriet thought, looking around. The floor plan was exactly like that of her own house. Stairs with a handsome curving banister rose to the right of the hall. To the left, where Harriet's living room was—where just the night before she had sat glumly while her parents told her she was not going with them to Paris—there was a heavy, closed mahogany door. On it a small brass plaque said MORRIS FEIGENBAUM, M.D.

Harriet tiptoed to the closed door and laid her left ear against it. From inside she could hear a low murmur: a woman's voice. Yammer yammer yammer. Harriet couldn't make out the words, but they sounded like complaints. The voice sounded like her mother's friend Sylvia Connelly, who complained frequently. "So I took it back to Lord and Taylor and told them that *never* in my *life* had I been sold such shoddy merchandise. . . . And the headmaster, well, they call him the commandant, called me and said that Malcolm had been disruptive, and I said, 'Sir! This boy is an angel at home, and if he isn't an angel at your school, well, I would look to the environment. . . .' So I bid four hearts, which *should* have been a closeout, but that idiot said four spades, and . . ."

Yammer yammer. It wasn't Sylvia Connelly behind the door, Harriet knew, because Sylvia Connelly was at her stupid apartment on Fifth Avenue, yammering on the telephone to Harriet's mother. But it *sounded* like Sylvia Connelly, and Harriet felt very sorry for Morris Feigenbaum because he had to listen.

"Who is it?" The same voice she had heard through the speaker, the receptionist's voice, called down the stairs. Harriet noticed now that there was another brass plaque, this one saying BARBARA FEIGENBAUM, M.D., on the wall beside the staircase, and there was a small arrow pointing up. Fearful that the receptionist would lean over the railing and look down into the hall, Harriet scurried to the rear of the hallway and stood behind a large antique cabinet at the top of the stairs that she knew from her own house's identical geography led to the kitchen. She took out her notebook.

HEADING DOWN TO KITCHEN WHERE STRANGER WAS SEEN. THESE MAY BE MY LAST WORDS.

She stood silently for a moment, aware that these were not very interesting last words. She tried to think of one of Ole Golly's meaningful quotations. The one that came to mind seemed completely suitable and she wrote the words at the end of her will with satisfaction.

PEOPLE WHO LOVE THEIR WORK LOVE LIFE.
SIGNED: HARRIET M. (FOR MIDDLE) WELSCH, SPY

Harriet replaced her notebook in her pocket and began to inch forward. When, moving stealthily, she was partway down the stairs to the kitchen, she heard footsteps below her, and the opening of a door.

"Here, kitty kitty," a girl's voice called.

Harriet waited.

"There you are, silly kitty," the girl crooned. "Come in." The door closed and Harriet heard footsteps again.

Suddenly, before she had time to hide in the shadows, Harriet was confronted by a ponytailed girl at the foot of the stairs. She was holding the gray-and-white cat from the yard and was staring in surprise at Harriet.

"Who are *you?*" the girl asked.

Harriet drew herself up. "Private investigator," she said in an authoritative voice. "I heard reports of a home invasion taking place at this address. Just checking. Everything all right here?"

"Private investigator, my foot. You're no older than I am."

"I'm a spy," Harriet said defiantly.

"And I'm a transvestite movie star."

"Hah."

"Double hah."

The two girls stared at each other. The cat began to wriggle in the ponytailed girl's arms. She tried to clasp it more tightly but its wriggling increased and it meowed.

"Scratch it under the chin, gently," Harriet suggested.

"You think you know everything about cats?"

"Well, I know about *this* cat," Harriet said. "And you don't seem to." The girl frowned and scratched the cat under its chin. The cat stretched and began to purr.

"Who are you, anyway?" the girl asked.

"My name's Harriet M. Welsch. I'm a spy. I told you that already but you don't seem to listen. I live across the street. Who are you?"

"Is someone down there?" the receptionist's voice called down the stairs.

"Just me, talking to the cat!" the girl called back.

They could hear the receptionist climbing the stairs back to the second floor.

"They'll kill you if they catch you in here. You'd better go out the back door," the strange girl told Harriet. "It's over this way." She gestured.

"I know where it is," Harriet replied haughtily. "I know the entire floor plan of this house. Storage area over there, right?" She pointed to a small door off the kitchen.

"Think you're smart?"

"*Know* I'm smart," Harriet retorted. She went to the back door. "Who are you? I told you who *I* am."

"My name is Camilla Languid and I am terminally ill," the girl said. "My parents can't deal with the pain and grief and so I am living with my doctor until my demise, which is imminent. I may die this afternoon."

"You don't even look sick," Harriet said. She stepped through the back door, which Camilla Languid had unlocked and was holding open for her.

"I'm on steroids. I expect to live until next week, actually."

Harriet didn't know what to say. She hadn't known a dying person before. Well, once maybe. A homeless man who had often slept under the front steps of a house around the corner. Harriet had gotten to know him fairly well. Then one day he was drunk and was hit by a bus on Madison Avenue and died. So technically, she figured, when she knew him he was a dying person. But it wasn't quite the same.

"I'm very sorry," Harriet said politely. "I hope to see you again before . . ." She didn't know how to finish the sentence, so her voice trailed off awkwardly. She moved across the yard toward the gate and waved to the girl, who stood in the doorway watching her.

As she let herself out and pulled the gate closed behind her, Harriet heard the girl call loudly, "You didn't believe that, did you?"

"Believe what?"

"All that crud about me being terminally ill? You stupe!"

"Of course I didn't," Harriet lied. "You didn't believe that crud about me being a spy, did you?"

"No. What do you think I am, a jerk?"

Yes, Harriet thought, but decided not to say.

"I'm actually a juvenile delinquent," the girl called. "My name is Rosarita Sauvage and I'm under house arrest. I wear an electronic anklet."

Harriet opened the gate and poked her head through. "And I," she called back, "am actually named Harriet M. Welsch and I really *am* a spy. So watch out!"

With dignity Harriet closed the gate again and made her way home. She felt oddly disappointed. For a minute on seeing the girl with the ponytail she had thought that perhaps she would have a new friend living right across the street. Harriet would have liked that. She had friends at school, but none of them were truly what Harriet thought of as FOTHs, Friends of the Heart: the kind of people who shared her hopes and dreams. Her school friends seemed to share things like homework assignments and gossip, and those were things that didn't interest Harriet much. Sport was certainly a FOTH, but he was a boy, which mattered even though it shouldn't; also, he wasn't across the street.

"Telephone for you, dear," her mother called as she climbed the stairs.

"Who is it? Sport?"

"No, I think it's a girl. She sounds quite odd. I do hope you're not mixed up with unsavory people, Harriet."

Harriet rolled her eyes and answered the phone.

"H'spy?" the voice said. "Rosarita here."

"I told you, my name's Harriet."

"I'm calling you H'spy. People need secret names. H'spy can be yours."

"How do you spell it?"

"H-apostrophe-S-P-Y."

"It's weird. You can't put *H* and *S* together. Maybe if you're Chinese, but I'm not. And you don't put apostrophes in names."

"You can do whatever you want. In my last

school there were several people with apostrophes in their names. Q'aadara was one. I put an apostrophe in H'spy because I think you need it. It's nicely flamboyant."

"Spies aren't supposed to be flamboyant," Harriet pointed out, though actually she was beginning to like the idea of the apostrophe and was already picturing the unusual signature it could make. "Where do you go to school, anyway?"

Rosarita sighed. "I am about to enter a terrible school designed especially for miscreants and misfits. I won't speak its name aloud."

"How did you get my phone number? Why did you call me?" Harriet asked. "You said I was a stupe."

"You're the spy. It's easy to find a phone number if you know someone's name and address. Well, you live across the street. I thought we might have some sort of relationship."

"Like we could be friends?"

There was a silence. "That's going too far. Let's just say that we might meet occasionally to converse and compare notes."

"An infrequent meeting or conversation might be nice," Harriet agreed. She was not one to share her notes.

"I'm going to give you a telephone number. If

you call, let it ring once, then hang up. It's a signal. I'll call back and we'll arrange to meet."

Harriet wrote down the number. "All right," she said. "A dial-and-ditch. I can do that."

"G'bye, H'spy."

"Goodbye," Harriet said, and hung up the phone. For a moment she stood there, wondering whether she had a new friend or a new problem.

CHAPTER 4

Finally: Tuesday! Harriet's time line was spread out on her bedroom floor, and she was working on the events of the past several days. But it was difficult to concentrate. Every so often she stood up and looked through her front window down to the street below. She was watching for a taxi. Ole Golly was due any minute.

OLE GOLLY RETURNS. Harriet had written it in two places. First she had written it in her notebook. WE MUST NEVER SPEAK OF HER UNFORTUNATE MONTHS IN MONTREAL, she had added as a reminder and an instruction to herself. Of course, that meant the time in Montreal would remain a mystery. And to Harriet, to a spy like Harriet, mysteries cried out to be solved.

She would have to curb her spying-and-solving impulse. She could hardly, however, control her curiosity.

A NEW CHAPTER OF OUR LIFE TOGETHER BEGINS, she had written finally across the top of a fresh page before putting the notebook away.

Then she had written the same headline—OLE GOLLY RETURNS—in highly decorated letters on the next-to-last page of her time line. Many pages before, she could see OLE GOLLY ARRIVES as the major news from her earliest days; then, not so very far back, OLE GOLLY MARRIES AND MOVES TO MONTREAL was printed in somber penmanship, the way an obituary might be written.

Other news would be added on this current page. BEGINS SEVENTH GRADE would appear in another two weeks. But for now the return of Catherine Golly was top headline, even though (Harriet looked again impatiently) no taxi had appeared yet.

"Dear?" Her mother called from a lower floor. "Cook says lunch is almost ready."

Harriet unweighted the time line and let it curl itself into a cylinder. She went across the small hallway to be certain once again that everything was ready. She had announced on Saturday afternoon that she planned to repaint Ole Golly's room to spruce up the brightness of its yellow walls, but Harriet's parents reminded her that they had had the room professionally repainted after Ole Golly moved out because they planned to use it as a guest room. They had paid eight hundred dollars, they said, to a painter named Brian Cleary, and the room had not been used since. That had been only about ten months ago.

So Harriet had decided she didn't want to repaint the room anyway. But she did want the room to look special. She bought yellow flowers at a store around the corner and placed them in a small blue pitcher. They were still upright and fresh on Ole Golly's bureau. Beside them was a small dish of chocolate kisses. Harriet had a feeling that perhaps while they were eating the candy together, the subject of kisses in general could be brought up and the topic of love introduced without mentioning Mr. Waldenstein's name.

She had gone downstairs to the library and selected books she knew were Ole Golly's favorites: Dostoievsky, Wordsworth, and *Shakespeare: The Complete Plays*, which was very thick and heavy and full of footnotes. Those books were neatly stacked on the table beside the rocking chair. Harriet had added her paperback Scrabble dictionary to the pile, along with a Hallmark card that said GOOD LUCK IN YOUR NEW HOME. The card had a picture of a small cottage with a thatched roof and smoke curling from its chimney—not exactly the right kind of picture, but it was the only new-home card Harriet could find at the corner pharmacy. Carefully she had signed it, after a long period of thought, *No nonsense, Harriet the Spy.*

She lifted a corner of the bedspread and determined that the clean sheets were still clean. She opened the door of the closet and determined that the neat row of empty wooden coat hangers was still hanging in an orderly way. She turned on all the lamps to be certain that no lightbulbs needed replacing, and then she turned them all off again. Finally she examined the framed print of Van Gogh's *Sunflowers* that had always hung on the yellow wall opposite the window. Harriet took out her retractable tape measure and determined that the frame was askew by a sixteenth of an inch. Carefully she straightened it. Then she looked around the room one more time, decided it was perfect, and headed down the stairs for lunch just as the taxi pulled up to the Welsches' front door.

● ● ●

Harriet burst through the door and dashed down the front steps to the sidewalk. Ole Golly was leaning into the cab having an argument with the driver.

" 'He that filches from me my good name robs me of that which not enriches him,' " she was saying in a firm, somewhat arrogant, slightly angry voice. She handed the driver some money.

"What's that, a fortune cookie message?" the taxi driver asked sarcastically.

"I am waiting for my change, young man. It's Shakespeare. Iago in act three, scene three of *Othello*. You would do well to improve your reading habits."

The driver gave her some coins. Ole Golly looked at them carefully. "And your driving habits, too," she said. "You were well over the speed limit until the light at Eighty-seventh Street."

The driver scowled, leaned over, slammed the door, and sped away, leaving Ole Golly standing beside her suitcase on the curb with the coins in her hand. Harriet threw her arms around her. It was not easy, because Ole Golly was—as she always had been—wrapped in layers of tweed, even in August. She was also wearing the sturdy, sensible shoes Harriet remembered and a rust-colored felt hat with a small feather, and she was carrying a large brown purse.

"You're back! You're back!"

"Disentangle yourself, Harriet. That man drove away without waiting for his tip, not that he deserved one." Ole Golly put the coins into her purse. "Please be so kind as to help me with my valise."

"I have so much to tell you! My parents are going to France! Well, of course, you know that already, don't you? What else? Oh yes, Sport's father got married, imagine that! I *cannot* figure out why! But his wife is nice and lets Sport cook! Oh dear, I'm sorry, maybe I shouldn't speak of marriage—"

Harriet struggled up the front steps with the heavy suitcase. Ole Golly was greeting her parents in the front hall, the three of them quite businesslike and polite.

"I'm making a time line, and you're on it! And school starts very soon. I think my homeroom teacher will be Mr. Grenville. Remember him? He's the one who did an Elvis imitation at the teachers' assembly last year. I told you about it. It was *so* bad. And guess what, Ole Golly, Sport said he would make some oatmeal cookies, your favorite, and he's bringing them over this afternoon! And—"

But no one was listening, and Harriet realized she was yammering. Cook was calling from the foot of the stairs that lunch was getting cold, Mrs.

Welsch was describing the apartment in Paris, Ole Golly was saying in a huff that New York taxi drivers were even worse than they had been last time she was here, and Mr. Welsch was glancing at the folded newspaper in his hand and saying something about interest rates and the Federal Reserve. They were *all* yammering. It didn't matter. Happily Harriet set the suitcase down on the hall floor and followed everyone into the dining room for lunch.

· · ·

"See? OLE GOLLY RETURNS. Isn't the penmanship wonderful? I used an Ultra Fine Sharpie. This is the most current, up-to-date part of my time line," Harriet was explaining to Sport.

"Why aren't I on it? Couldn't you add SIMON ROCQUE BRINGS OATMEAL COOKIES?"

They were sprawled on the bedroom floor. Across the hall Ole Golly was unpacking. They could hear her feet moving across the room from suitcase to closet. They could hear the wooden coat hangers being lifted, arranged, and replaced.

"Not important enough. You have to get a sense of what's important, Sport. The only things that you put on a time line are things that might change the course of events to come. Oatmeal cookies have never, ever done that."

"The invention of gunpowder has."

"Yes, that would be one. I would have put that on if I were doing the whole world."

"The Black Plague."

"Yes, that, too. *If* I were doing the world."

"Starting seventh grade."

"Now you're getting it. That affects *my* part of the world. I'll put that on when it happens. And I did put MATTHEW ROCQUE GETS MARRIED. But that should really have gone on *your* time line, if you had one, Sport, because he's *your* father."

"Starting seventh grade would go on mine, too," Sport pointed out. Harriet noticed that he had a glum expression on his face.

"Are you worried about going to a new school?" she asked him. Privately she had been worrying a lot on his behalf.

"No." But Harriet, trained observer that she was, could tell that it was a *no* filled with bravado and that Sport was actually very nervous at the prospect of attending such a large school. She didn't blame him. The Gregory School, which she and Sport had both gone to for years, was so small and intimate it was like a family—with the quarrels and quirks (Ah! Two Q words for Scrabble, Harriet realized with pleasure) of a family, but like a family, there were hugs and jokes and a lot of shared memories, too.

Now for Sport school would be complete strangeness, among people who wouldn't understand him. It would be like living in a foreign country. It would be like—

"Ole Golly?" Harriet called suddenly. The footsteps paused in the yellow bedroom across the hall. "Can you come here?"

Ole Golly appeared in Harriet's bedroom door and looked down at Harriet and Sport. She had taken off some of her layers of tweed after lunch, and now she was down to a voluminous jumper over a white blouse clasped at the neck with a thick gold brooch. With her hat off, her familiar hair, bunched in the back into the unfashionable bun Harriet had always loved, was visible.

Ole Golly frowned at them. "Might I remind you that *bellowing* is a less than effective way to summon someone?"

"You *did* bellow, Harriet," Sport said. "Anything louder than a politely raised voice *is* a bellow."

"Sorry," Harriet sighed. She was thinking that

bellow might go on her list of strong verbs, to which she had just that morning added a new favorite: *lunge*. She looked up at Ole Golly.

"I just wanted to ask you something, because Sport and I were talking about school. He's going to a new school this fall, Ole Golly, and it won't be at all like the Gregory School. In fact, it might even be populated with hoodlums and criminals, so of course he's scared blue—"

"I didn't say any of that, Harriet," Sport told her angrily. "I didn't say one bit of it."

"I read minds."

Sport glared at her but couldn't think of a retort because he knew it was true. Harriet *could* read his mind.

"Anyway," Harriet went on, ignoring Sport's glare, "since you have quite recently done the same thing, Ole Golly—"

"Meaning what, exactly?" Now Ole Golly was glaring, too.

"Meaning you left a very familiar, comfortable place and went off to a new and different place, which you knew nothing about—"

"About which," Ole Golly corrected. But she was still glaring.

"Whatever. And you probably didn't know what to expect, the way Sport doesn't, and were very nervous, the way Sport is—"

"I never said that," Sport reminded her.

Harriet shot him a withering glance. Had he perhaps forgotten that she was able to read minds?

"So," Harriet continued, "I thought you might be able to give him some heartening advice."

Ole Golly simply stared at her.

"Well," Harriet pointed out, "he *did* make you those cookies."

"They were excellent, Simon," Ole Golly said, looking at Sport. "And I *am* concerned for you, starting out on this new and perhaps frightening enterprise."

"Heartening advice," Harriet whispered loudly to her as a reminder.

"Be aware," Ole Golly said to Sport after a pause, "that things are not always what they seem. Adjustments must be made. But somehow we manage to muddle through."

Muddle? Not a very strong verb, Harriet thought. And not particularly heartening.

" '*Thanks to the human heart by which we live,*' " Ole Golly concluded. "That's a quote from Wordsworth. Bear it in mind." She turned to go back to her room.

"Harriet," she said over her shoulder, "I need three more coat hangers. They need not be wood. And a one-hundred-watt bulb for the lamp beside the chair where I read. Sixty watts is inadequate for reading."

When she had gone, Harriet and Sport sat together silently for a moment. "She's changed," Sport said at last. "Something's different about her."

Harriet was thinking the same thing, though she didn't want it to be true. She wanted absolutely nothing to be changed about Ole Golly. "Her hair?" she suggested. "It's a little different, I think."

Sport shook his head. "Something more on the inside. She seems sad."

Harriet stared at him, knowing he was right. Ole Golly *did* seem sad, and just at the time when Harriet felt so happy. Harriet didn't want Ole Golly to be sad, ever. She chewed on her lower lip, something she often did when she was thinking. Then she marched into Ole Golly's room.

"What's the matter with you?" Harriet demanded. It needed to be asked.

"You may knock before entering my room," Ole Golly replied evenly. She was sitting in her chair, staring out the window. No book, no knitting, just staring.

Knock? thought Harriet. That's a new rule. But Harriet was good at following rules. When she felt like it, at least.

"Is something wrong? Besides the lightbulb and the coat hangers?" Harriet tried again.

" 'Alas, how easily things go wrong! A sigh too much, or a kiss too long.' "

"What?"

"George Macdonald."

"Why are you acting so strange?" Harriet was getting exasperated. She didn't like having to repeat herself.

"I just need some time alone, Harriet. Everyone does. Even you and Sport. Right now you are spending your time together. So I will take some time alone. Now if you don't mind . . ."

And with that, Harriet turned on her heel and showed herself out. But she purposely left the door open so Ole Golly would have to get up from her chair to close it if she wanted to be completely alone.

"Since when does Ole Golly need time to herself?" she asked Sport. "She's here to take care of me, after all. That is why she lives here, in my house, across the hall from my room, sharing my phone."

Then something else caught Harriet's attention.

"Sport?" Harriet said, leaning forward. "Look up

there toward the window. Lean your head that way. I need to examine your face."

Sport frowned, but he obeyed, raising his face toward the light of the window.

"I think . . ." Harriet took her magnifying glass from her pocket. She held it to Sport's upper lip. "Yes, it's true."

"*What's* true?" Sport asked suspiciously. He pulled away from her scrutiny.

"Hairs. Growing between your mouth and nose."

"*Hairs?*"

"At least four. Maybe five."

Harriet put the magnifying glass back in her pocket and picked up her pencil. She began to write something just below OLE GOLLY RETURNS. "This puts you in my time line, Sport. Oatmeal cookies didn't do it, but this does. This will certainly affect the course of future events."

"What do you mean, *this?*" Sport crouched down and squinted to see what Harriet was writing so neatly.

SIMON ROCQUE ENTERS PUBERTY

Sport fingered his upper lip in dismay. Harriet underlined the sentence and they both stared at it.

Across the hall they heard Ole Golly sit down in the rocking chair. They heard her give a deep sigh, as if disappointment had moved into the yellow room with her.

"Did she say something?" Sport whispered to Harriet. Harriet shook her head.

"It was just a sigh," she whispered. "She never used to sigh. She considered sighing a waste of breath."

Harriet released the time line so that it rolled itself up again and made space on the floor of her room.

"Harriet," Sport said, "I gotta go. I'm making a pot roast for dinner and it has to go into the oven by four."

"Send out for Chinese," Harriet ordered. "This is more important."

"No, I'm going," Sport said firmly. "Bye, Ole Golly!" he called a little nervously, and headed for the stairs.

"I have to shave," he told Harriet, and off he went, leaving her alone, across from the yellow room with the now tightly closed door and the puzzling sound of sighs.

CHAPTER 5

Harriet kept the Feigenbaums' house under almost constant surveillance from her bedroom window. She used the small binoculars that her parents took for bird-watching every time they were invited to the Connellys' summer home on Nantucket. Harriet had gone with them for one of those weekends, but she hadn't enjoyed it much. Malcolm and Edmund Connelly had been there, and they kept reciting a limerick about Nantucket that Harriet had not wanted to hear.

But she was glad now of the bird-watching binoculars. She sat in her desk chair, which she had moved near the window, and watched the Feigenbaums' house. She thought that if she saw Rosarita in a window, she might wave in a casually friendly way.

People who looked like patients came and went, each of them ringing the bell and speaking into the intercom beside the door as Harriet had. The door opened and closed again and again, and Harriet carefully noted the activity in her notebook.

TALL PREGNANT WOMAN, BAD HAIR DAY, ARRIVES BY CAB, ENTERS HOUSE 9:55 A.M. LEAVES 11 A.M., KLEENEX CLUTCHED IN HAND, WALKS TO CORNER, DISAPPEARS.
OVERWEIGHT MAN WEARING BLUE SHORT-SLEEVED SHIRT, CARRYING NEWSPAPER, ARRIVES 2 P.M., ENTERS HOUSE, LEAVES 2:45 P.M., APPEARS INDECISIVE, THEN WALKS WEST TOWARD PARK. NO LONGER CARRYING PAPER.

Her notes and her observations were meticulous. They were also, Harriet realized after a while, boring. But spies on surveillance were often required to do boring things. Harriet yawned. Perhaps things would be more stimulating outside.

Still no action at the Feigenbaums'. Sitting on her front stoop, she turned to the Ole Golly section of her notebook.

SOMETHING IS WRONG WITH OLE GOLLY. SHE USED TO SAY THAT PEOPLE WHO DON'T DO ANYTHING DON'T THINK ANYTHING, SO THERE'S NOTHING TO THINK ABOUT THEM. BUT NOW IT'S OLE GOLLY WHO DOESN'T DO OR SAY ANY-THING. SHE SITS AND STARES. I DID THAT FOR A LITTLE WHILE LAST YEAR AFTER SHE LEFT. AT FIRST I DIDN'T READ OR DO MY MATH. I EVEN NEGLECTED MY SPY ROUTE—BUT ONLY FOR A SHORT PERIOD. IS THAT WHY OLE GOLLY WANTS TO BE ALONE ALL THE TIME? IS SHE SAD?

She wrote carefully on a new page:

SUGGESTIONS FOR POSSIBLY CHEERING UP OLE GOLLY

She underlined it. Harriet didn't often underline things. But she felt an urgency in this list. She got up and repositioned herself on the Rhinelanders' front steps four houses down the street, within view of her own house, and thought. Nothing much came to mind at first, so she carefully gave the title a spastic colon by placing two dots vertically after the word *Golly* so that it became GOLLY:.

(It was really only an ordinary colon. But Harriet had once overheard her father talking about a net-work executive named Mr. Alfred Lancaster who had a spastic colon. She liked the sound of the phrase. Now whenever she made two vertical dots, she thought spastic colon. It gave a sense of importance to punctuation that was otherwise completely undistinguished.)

She began to make the list.

1. WATCH A MOVIE TOGETHER, BUT NOT ONE THAT HAS ANYTHING TO DO WITH OLE GOLLY'S RECENT PAST.

2. DISCUSS BOOKS, BUT NOT ANY THAT HAVE TO DO WITH OLE GOLLY'S RECENT PAST.

3. JOIN AN EXERCISE CLASS AT THE 92ND STREET Y. OR MAYBE YOGA. (WOULD OLE GOLLY DO THIS? PROBABLY NOT. SHE DOES NOT LIKE TO EXHIBIT HER BODY.)

4. OH LORD, INVITE SYLVIA CONNELLY OVER FOR LUNCH. (ONLY IF MALCOLM AND EDMUND ARE NOT IN TOWN BE-CAUSE IF SHE BROUGHT THEM IT WOULD BE UNBEARABLE. IT WOULD BE UNBEARABLE ANYWAY.)

5. TAKE HER TO SAKS FIFTH AVENUE AND MAKE SCATHING REMARKS ABOUT THE CLOTHES. (SOMETIMES OLE GOLLY IS WILLING TO DO THIS.)

6. DISTRIBUTE SANDWICHES TO HOMELESS PEOPLE AND URGE THEM GENTLY AND UNJUDGMENTALLY TO PULL THEMSELVES TOGETHER.

7. VISIT A FORTUNE-TELLER.

But even after the list was complete, Harriet didn't feel any better about the situation. By the time she finished this entry, there had still been no glimpse of the strange girl in the Feigenbaums' house.

● ● ●

Her parents had left for Paris with a flurry of last-minute instructions and an assortment of luggage that required them to take two separate taxis to the airport. They had arrived safely in France and had telephoned the next day.

"*Bonjour!* It's three P.M. here!" her mother had announced excitedly into the phone. "What time is it there?"

"Nine A.M.," Harriet told her. "I'm still eating breakfast. I'm sitting in the kitchen."

"Oh!" her mother said, as if breakfast were exciting. "What are you having?"

"Cornflakes and banana. I ordered Belgian waffles with fresh strawberries but Cook told me to go soak my head."

"It's raining here! What is it doing there?"

Harriet glanced through the window. "Nothing. A little cloudy."

"And Ole Golly's all right?"

"I guess." She would never tell her parents. Harriet had decided that whatever was deeply troubling Ole Golly, she would deal with it alone. A spy's life was very often solitary.

"I'll call again in a few days! Kiss kiss!" That was her mother's telephone way of saying goodbye. Harriet sighed, said a normal goodbye to her mother, hung up the phone, and went back to her last bit of cornflakes. Cook, at the sink, glanced over.

"Yammer yammer," Harriet said, and shrugged.

"You wait. She'll be yammering in French pretty soon."

"I don't mind. I speak French. I learned it in school."

"How do you say *cornflakes with banana?*" Cook asked, taking Harriet's empty bowl to the sink.

Harriet thought. "We didn't learn that yet," she said finally. "But this is *la table*." She pointed to the wooden kitchen table. "My cornflakes were *sur la table*. You can see I'm pretty fluent."

"How do you say *Your cornflakes are all gone and I want to clean the kitchen and you're in the way?*" Cook asked, standing with a sponge poised over the table.

Harriet pondered the question. "I would tell you," she said, "but you are too mean and sarcastic.

72

Tell me, Cook, do you belong to the Mean and Sarcastic Club of Brooklyn?"

"Yes," Cook replied. "I'm president. Move your butt out of that chair."

"I could say that in French if I wished," Harriet told her, and left the kitchen. *"Au revoir,"* she called breezily from the stairs.

Up in her room again, Harriet went straight for her notebook and turned to the Ole Golly section.

THINGS THAT COULD BE MAKING OLE GOLLY SAD:

1. COOK'S BAD ATTITUDE

2. THE DECLINE OF THE NOVEL IN WESTERN CIVILIZATION (Harriet had heard Ole Golly mention this on several occasions.)

3. THE MYSTERIOUS HAPPENINGS IN MONTREAL THAT LED HER TO RESUME HER POST IN THE WELSCH HOUSEHOLD

4. SOMETHING I HAVE DONE

Using her deductive reasoning, Harriet concluded that number 3 was the most likely cause (closely followed by number 1 and number 2. Number 4 seemed highly unlikely to Harriet).

WHY HAS OLE GOLLY RETURNED TO NEW YORK ALONE? WHERE IS GEORGE WALDENSTEIN? WHY WOULD SHE

RETURN ALONE IF IT MADE HER SAD? SHE SHOULD HAVE
JUST BROUGHT HIM WITH HER. THE YELLOW BEDROOM IS
ONLY SLIGHTLY SMALLER THAN MY OWN AND COULD EAS-
ILY ACCOMMODATE TWO PEOPLE. OLE GOLLY WOULD NOT
HAVE RETURNED WITHOUT HER HUSBAND UNLESS THERE
WAS NO ALTERNATIVE.

Harriet came up with only one possible conclu-
sion.

GEORGE WALDENSTEIN WOULD BE INCAPABLE OF RETURN-
ING TO NEW YORK ONLY IF HE IS DECEASED.

Harriet looked at the words and immediately
knew they were true. It was nothing less than a
tragedy. Granted, Harriet had not cared for George
Waldenstein immediately. Upon first meeting him,
he had seemed much too obvious. And why had a
grown man still been a delivery boy anyway? But
she had come around quickly. George Waldenstein
was quite different from the other adults she had
known—just like Ole Golly. They really had been a
perfect match. Harriet was crestfallen at the news.
(What exactly did *crestfallen* mean? How does a crest
fall and why would anyone care if it did?)

No wonder Ole Golly was sad. It was like *Romeo and Juliet*, only completely different.

Words from Harriet's favorite poem came to her mind, so she wrote them in her notebook.

"I WEEP FOR YOU," THE WALRUS SAID:
"I DEEPLY SYMPATHIZE."
WITH SOBS AND TEARS HE SORTED OUT
THOSE OF THE LARGEST SIZE,
HOLDING HIS POCKET-HANDKERCHIEF
BEFORE HIS STREAMING EYES.

* * *

Ole Golly spoke French, as well. Harriet had discovered this piece of information one evening when she mentioned to Ole Golly that she had met someone with an unusual name. Harriet didn't want to explain that she had actually entered the Feigenbaums' house under what might be called false pretenses. So she simply said, "I have met someone with an unusual name."

"And that would be?"

"Rosarita Sauvage," Harriet said.

They were in Ole Golly's bedroom after dinner. The chocolate kisses were all gone, and Harriet had not found a way to bring up the topic of kissing tactfully. She decided she would buy more and try again.

Ole Golly was casting blue stitches onto a long knitting needle. She was starting a sweater for Harriet. Harriet had chosen the pattern out of a knitting book: blue with yellow stripes and an occasional red starlike shape. It looked very difficult. But Ole Golly said it wasn't.

"Stand here for a minute with your back to me." Ole Golly took her tape measure and stretched it across the back of Harriet's shoulders. Harriet held her arms out like a scarecrow and hoped the tape measure wouldn't touch her armpits. She was very ticklish there.

"Rosareeeeeeta Sauvaaaaage," she repeated, dragging the sounds out as if she were playing them on an oboe. It seemed a very mysterious name.

Ole Golly rolled up the tape measure and went back to the knitting needles. She began to count stitches.

"Rosareeeeeeta Sauvaaaaage," Harriet intoned again.

"Shhhhh. Thirty-nine, forty, forty-one . . ."

Finally Ole Golly finished counting. She stabbed

the needles into the ball of yarn and placed it in her knitting basket at the foot of the rocking chair. "Fierce," she said. "Untamed."

Harriet frowned. "I don't think so. Maybe if it had big patches of different colors on it, it would be sort of untamed. But a few stripes and those little star things, that's fairly ordinary. Beth Ellen Hansen has a sweater that her grandmother got in Norway, and it—"

"The name," Ole Golly said. "*Sauvage*. Or, as you apparently prefer to say it: Sau*vaaaaage*. That's French for *fierce*."

"No kidding! You speak French that well, that you can translate a name? I didn't know you could do that, Ole Golly! I thought I knew everything about you, but—"

"No one knows everything about another human being, Harriet. It is presumptuous to think so."

Harriet thought it over and realized Ole Golly was right. She kept learning new things about people every single day.

"You're right," she conceded. "Just this morning I learned that Cook is president of the Mean and Sarcastic Club of Brooklyn. And now I learn that you are bilingual. I wonder what other secrets you might be keeping from me." She looked meaningfully, sympathetically, knowingly at Ole Golly.

But Ole Golly, examining the knitting instructions, only said, "Are you sure you want those star shapes in red?"

Harriet sighed. "*Oui,*" she said, remembering her sixth-grade French. "*Rouge.*"

"All right then. *Rouge,* to go with the *bleu* and the *jaune.*" Ole Golly poked through the basket of yarns and took out a small skein of red. "Hold this," she directed, "while I wind it into a ball."

Dutifully Harriet put the skein of red yarn over her hands and held them slightly apart. She had been doing this for years and was quite experienced at it now; she knew just how to hold the yarn taut and move her hands slightly as Ole Golly wound it into a ball.

"How did you learn French? Did they teach it in school in Far Rockaway? How do you say *knitting* in French?"

"*Tricotage,* I think. And no, I did not learn French in Far Rockaway. The only things I learned in Far Rockaway were roller-skating, penmanship, and a passionate wish to flee."

"But how—"

"I've been living for some months in Montreal,

remember. You pick up a lot of French if you live in Montreal."

Ah! thought Harriet. A conversational opening! Carefully she considered how to make use of it.

"I suppose," she began in a casual voice, "that one might pick up a lot of things in Montreal."

"One might." The little red ball of yarn was growing in Ole Golly's hands as she wound it with exactness.

Harriet thought. She wanted to say, "A fatal illness, perhaps?" And from there Ole Golly would tell all, would reveal the death of George Waldenstein, her own huge, unassuageable grief, and her decision to return to the home where she had once been happy and carefree. But Harriet felt it would be unseemly to mention the death, particularly since she had been forbidden to mention Mr. Waldenstein's name to Ole Golly. She had to make her way toward it gradually.

"One might pick up a taste for French cooking, I suppose."

"Yes. *La cuisine*. One might, indeed," Ole Golly replied.

Harriet tried to picture how it might have happened. She pictured George Waldenstein as she had known him: balding, with a mustache, a shy, formal smile, and a pudgy, roly-poly, Pillsbury Doughboy body. He did love to eat, Harriet knew. Often during their courtship Mr. Waldenstein and Ole Golly had gone to restaurants in the neighborhood for dinner.

Perhaps he had simply eaten too much and his stomach had burst and he had died.

Harriet thought of French food words she knew. Many of the vocabulary words in fifth- and sixth-grade French had been food words.

"I imagine that in Montreal one might be tempted to eat too many *haricots verts* and *pommes frites* and *marrons glacés* and *gâteaux* and then one could get a terrible stomachache or appendicitis."

Ole Golly didn't reply.

"And you could die."

Ole Golly frowned at Harriet in a puzzled but unperturbed way and still didn't reply.

Maybe, Harriet thought, it wasn't simple over-eating that had killed George Waldenstein. Maybe it was food poisoning. A bad piece of fish could do it.

She moved her hands and the yarn continued to unwind. Or maybe it was *murder*, Harriet thought. Yet unsolved. That would cause a lot of sighing.

Harriet tried to think of a way to approach the subject tactfully and in a roundabout manner. Spies were good at getting information by such means.

"Sometimes," Harriet said, "it is very hard to accept the loss of a loved one if you don't know exactly *why* it happened, and maybe you keep thinking you could have prevented it, like, oh, let me see, in this book I read once, I forget the title, about a woman— well, actually, she was a mermaid—anyway, she was deeply in love with—"

To her astonishment, Ole Golly stopped winding the yarn. She looked stricken. Then she whipped the remaining strand of red from Harriet's outstretched hands.

"Enough," she said tersely. "Thank you for your help. Please go and take your bath."

"But—"

"Just *go. Va t'en. Vite.*"

Harriet did. Obediently she turned on the water to fill the tub. Then, while she waited, she took out her notebook and wrote.

GEORGE WALDENSTEIN WAS MURDERED IN MONTREAL. IT WAS PROBABLY A DARK AND STORMY NIGHT BUT WE DO NOT KNOW FOR SURE. OLE GOLLY'S DEEP GRIEF WILL NEVER

BE CURED UNTIL SHE KNOWS THE ANSWERS. THIS WILL
TAKE ~~PRECEDENTS~~ ~~PRECEDNE~~ PRESIDENCE OVER ALL MY
OTHER ONGOING CASES.

Later, sitting in the tub with her elbows on her
knees, a good thinking position, Harriet wondered
whether it would be a wise move to consult the
Canadian authorities. She decided to wait.

CHAPTER 6

Walking home from school, Harriet hummed. Seventh grade had begun, and as she had expected, Mr. Grenville was her homeroom teacher. He was a pleasant man with a whimsical (yes, thought Harriet, great word: *whimsical*) sense of humor and a large wardrobe of cashmere sweaters. She wondered how he could afford them all. Teachers, she knew, didn't earn large salaries, and cashmere sweaters cost a lot of money. Her mother had a lot of them, and her father sometimes made remarks about the price.

"Red and yellow, green and blue . . . ," Harriet sang to herself, thinking of Mr. Grenville's sweater collection and recalling the song about the rainbow that her class had learned in kindergarten. *"All the*

colors that we know . . ." She waved to Fabio Dei Santi, driving past in his father's grocery truck with a cigarette dangling from his lips. He beeped the horn at her. The entire Dei Santi family felt that Fabio was going to come to *no good end,* but Harriet felt in her heart that they were mistaken. Of course, being a spy, she knew some things that they didn't know yet.

She knew, for example, that Fabio Dei Santi was in love with Marie Delatorre, who worked in a bakery on Third Avenue. It had taken a lot of lurking, but Harriet had finally seen Fabio and Marie kissing, on July 17 at about 5:15 P.M. She had written it down. It had been quite a serious kiss (ninety-two seconds, timed by her stopwatch) and Harriet suspected that it meant the end of two things: it was the end of Fabio's life of crime, the one his parents thought he was leading ("*Santa Maria,* what do I do to deserve a son like this, a school dropout, a bum?" Harriet had heard his mother say, wringing her hands in her apron); and it was also the end of Marie Delatorre's life in a convent, the one her parents hoped she would lead.

The whole concept of love fascinated Harriet. How did Fabio and Marie know they loved each other? How had it happened that their lives would change now and Fabio would become a husband and father instead of a car thief and con artist? Would it last for Fabio and Marie, the feeling that made them paste their lips together for ninety-two seconds? Harriet hoped so. She hoped that Marie Delatorre, probably soon to be Marie Dei Santi, would never end up alone and sighing, as Ole Golly had.

Harriet hoped that she would be invited to the wedding because she liked weddings, but if they didn't invite her, she planned to crash it. It was fairly easy to crash weddings; Harriet did it often. She simply put on her best dress, went into the church, and sat toward the back, looking like a distant cousin.

Receptions were harder to crash because they were usually some distance away, and people went there in cars and limos and taxis. Harriet didn't have any transportation, but that didn't matter. By walking she had crashed two wedding receptions at the Hotel Pierre, just to see what they were like. And she had decided that she liked wedding ceremonies, which were so wonderfully solemn, better than wedding receptions, which were frivolous.

Lately, though, Harriet had noticed an increasing tendency of the congregation to applaud at the end of a wedding ceremony. It was inappropriate. It was like cheering for God as if he were an NFL coach. Harriet did not believe very strongly in either God or the Jets, but she respected other people's beliefs and she did not think they should laugh and clap in church. She thought she might write a letter to *The New York Times* about it. Or perhaps she could phone the Pope.

Thinking about weddings, Harriet stopped on the corner, took out her notebook, and leaned against a mailbox to write a note under THINGS TO DO.

GET POPE'S TELEPHONE NUMBER FROM DIRECTORY ASSISTANCE.

She realized with some embarrassment that she couldn't remember the Pope's name. John? Pius? Once, she had read a list of all the popes in the entire history of the church, and now they were mixed up in her mind. She remembered there had been one named Innocent.

The name Innocent made her think of Ole Golly.

Ole Golly had been back in New York now for four weeks. She barely left the house. One afternoon, at Harriet's insistence, they had gone together to the Metropolitan Museum to see an exhibit of

Etruscan jewelry. But they had not stayed long, and Ole Golly had refused to go into the gift shop, a great disappointment to Harriet, who had hoped to charge a reproduction gold-filigree-and-semi-precious-stone neckband to her mother's account. (She thought she might go back to the museum on her own, especially if she received an invitation to the Dei Santi–Delatorre wedding. Her mother would want her to be properly attired for such an occasion, and Harriet thought the Etruscan neckband would go well with her blue vest and a white turtleneck.)

Surprisingly, Ole Golly had not called any of her old friends. But she had called her mother, Mrs. Golly, who still lived in Far Rockaway, several times.

Harriet had devoted a page in her notebook to Mrs. Golly a long time ago after Ole Golly had taken her there for a brief visit.

OLE GOLLY'S MOTHER LIVES IN A VERY SMALL AND VERY DIRTY HOUSE AND SHE SAYS "AIN'T" AND SHE THINKS BOOK-LEARNING IS A WASTE OF TIME. HOW DID SHE EVER HAVE OLE GOLLY?

And now, to her horror, Harriet had discovered through eavesdropping that Ole Golly planned to go live with Mrs. Golly in that filthy, unhappy house in December, after Harriet's parents returned.

"Thank you," she had heard Ole Golly say politely on the phone to Mrs. Welsch. "I do appreciate your generosity in offering. But I'll be moving on after you return.

"No," she went on after a moment, "it's not that I'm unhappy here. Harriet is a delight, as she always has been. And Cook and I have reached a *rapprochement*."

Harriet didn't know that word. Sitting in her cramped spying-and-eavesdropping position behind the door, she had written it hastily in her notebook and resolved to look it up.

Then, to her astonishment, she had heard Ole Golly say, "I'll be moving to my mother's in Far Rockaway."

Harriet was amazed. Ole Golly *hated* Far Rockaway! She didn't even like her mother very much!

She had watched as Ole Golly listened at the telephone. Mrs. Welsch was probably saying the same thing Harriet was thinking: "But you *hate* Far Rockaway! And you don't even like your mother!"

Then, at last, Ole Golly had whispered in an odd

voice—actually whispered, all the way to Paris—
"But you see, I realize I'm innocent."

Harriet had been stunned. It had never even occurred to her that Ole Golly might *not* be innocent!
A very large oversight for a spy. It was time to give
her complete focus to this case. Crouched in her
moving-while-spying stance, she had gone over to
her desk and resumed writing.

OLE GOLLY IS SAD BECAUSE GEORGE WALDENSTEIN IS
DEAD. OLE GOLLY DID NOT KILL GEORGE WALDENSTEIN. IT
WAS OBVIOUSLY AN ACCIDENT BUT NO ONE BELIEVES HER.
AND NOW SHE IS A FUGITIVE FROM JUSTICE.

SHE IS INNOCENT, Harriet added.

⁕ ⁕ ⁕

Later she discussed the notebook entry with Sport
and told him about the conversation she had overheard.

"Are you sure she said *innocent?*" Sport asked.
"Maybe she said *insane.* You'd have to be insane to
go live in Far Rockaway with Mrs. Golly." Sport had
met Ole Golly's mother, too.

"I have acute hearing," Harriet reminded him.

"It's true, the door was partially closed, but I feel certain she said 'I am innocent.' "

Sport shrugged. "Well, okay, maybe she did. But what if she *isn't*?"

"Isn't what?"

"What if she isn't innocent? What if she's just practicing saying it, for the police?"

"She *is* innocent. How can you even question that? We must help her," Harriet said firmly.

Now, walking home from school thinking about Ole Golly, approaching her house, Harriet saw the front door open.

As she watched, Ole Golly, dressed as always in layers of tweed and carrying her purse, came out.

Harriet drew back quickly so she was concealed by the half-dead arborvitae in a cement pot beside the wrought-iron railing on the Rhinelanders' steps. Harriet was adroit at making herself invisible, and she did it now, blending in with the greenery—or the brownish-greenery, in this case.

Stealthily she parted the brittle twigs of the sickly shrub and peered out. Ole Golly had turned and was walking purposefully down Eighty-sixth Street, away from the Rhinelanders' house, toward the corner. Harriet decided she would wait until it was safe and then follow.

Quickly she looked at her watch, turned the page in her notebook, and wrote:

THURSDAY, SEPTEMBER 26TH. 3:55 P.M. CATHERINE GOLLY LEAVES HOUSE, CARRYING PURSE AND

Harriet took her binoculars from her jacket pocket and focused on Ole Golly and what she was carrying in her left hand. She added:

SMALL PAPER BAG.

Harriet watched Ole Golly cross Eighty-sixth Street and prepared herself to follow once she disappeared around the corner. But to her amazement, Ole Golly began walking toward her, back the way she had come, but on the opposite side of the street. Of course! She had done what she had always taught Harriet to do: to cross at the corner. And now (Harriet ducked back behind the bush) she was walking in the opposite direction from the way she had started; and now—

Harriet blinked. Ole Golly was going up the Feigenbaums' front steps! She was ringing the bell! Speaking into the intercom! And then entering through the Feigenbaums' front door.

Now that Ole Golly had entered the house and couldn't see her, Harriet dashed down the street and up her own front steps and let herself in. She stood behind the draperies in the living room and peered through the window. From here she had an excellent view of the Feigenbaums'. She had been watching their house, looking fruitlessly for Rosarita, for ages, so she knew it by heart. Nothing ever changed. The curtains and window shades hung in the same positions day after day.

Harriet sighed. Surveillance was so boring. And it was time—*past* time, in fact—for the cake and milk Cook gave her every afternoon. She wondered if she dared to dash down to the kitchen for her snack.

Then she glanced at the telephone in the front hall and had an idea. She had memorized the number Rosarita had given her but had never tried to call. Now she dialed it carefully, let it ring once, and hung up. She waited.

Five minutes later the telephone rang. Harriet picked up the receiver and went into the living room. "Hello?" she said.

"H'spy?" Rosarita's voice was low.

"Yes. I haven't called till now because I was busy

with school starting." It seemed rather strange to be talking to someone who was in the same house Ole Golly had mysteriously entered. She wondered if Ole Golly might be sitting right there watching while Rosarita talked on the telephone. "Do you have company?" Harriet asked.

"No. I am alone. You wish to meet? We can set up a time and place."

Harriet looked at her watch. "Can you come over? Our cook always serves milk and cake about now."

She could hear the withering disdain in Rosarita's voice. "You've mistaken me for someone who likes social events," she said. "You go ahead and have your little snack. I will meet you when you're finished. Five P.M. in the alley, behind the trash cans.

"I can see you, by the way," Rosarita added. "You're in your living room, holding a beige telephone receiver to your right ear. Your glasses are crooked."

"I've been watching *your* house with binoculars, and I can't see *you!*" Harriet stretched the phone cord and ran to the window. But the Feigenbaums' windows were all still dark and empty.

"I'm fiendishly clever," Rosarita replied.

"Are you on the roof?"

"I'm looking now at the watch on your left wrist. The second hand is passing the eight. Now the nine."

"Are you behind a bush?"

"I'll see you at five," Rosarita said.

Harriet sighed. "Yes, all right, five," she said. "G'bye, H'spy."

*   *   *

"Harriet! Is that you up there?" Cook was calling from the kitchen.

"No, it's Scarlett O'Hara!" Harriet called back. "I'm up here designing a ball gown."

"Very funny, ha ha ha. Your milk is getting warm sitting here."

That did it. Harriet loathed warm milk. She glanced once more at the Feigenbaums' house, where nothing had changed. She replaced the binoculars in her pocket, returned the telephone to the hall table, and went down to the kitchen. At least she could use the time for an interrogation, she decided. Carefully she opened her notebook beside the plate of chocolate cake.

THURSDAY, 4:12 P.M. INTERROGATION OF COOK:

Q: DO YOU KNOW WHERE OLE GOLLY WENT A LITTLE WHILE AGO?

A: NONE OF YOUR BEESWAX.

Harriet put her pencil down and frowned at Cook. "It *is* my beeswax," she said. "She's supposed to be taking care of me, after all. But she's left the house, unexcused."

Cook was having cake as well. She licked some frosting from her lips. "You're twelve years old, Harriet," she said.

"Not quite."

"Well, pretty soon you will be. That's half grown. You don't need taking care of every minute."

"True. But I'm worried about Ole Golly. Also, this is an official interrogation, so you have to answer."

"What do you mean, official?"

"Look." Harriet slid the notebook across the table so Cook could see the title INTERROGATION OF COOK, followed by a spastic colon.

Cook frowned. "Is this more of that spy stuff, Harriet?" she asked suspiciously.

"Yes. Completely official."

"If I answer one question, will you let me get back to my work?"

"One question is all I have for you," Harriet promised.

"Oh, all right. Ask me again, then."

Harriet picked up her pen and began the interrogation a second time.

Q: DO YOU KNOW WHERE MISS CATHERINE GOLLY IS CURRENTLY LOCATED AND WHY?

A: YEAH, SHE'S ACROSS THE STREET FOR A DOCTOR'S APPOINTMENT.

"Cooky! Thank you!" Harriet closed her notebook and gulped the rest of her milk. "Of course! I should have figured that out for myself!"

She ate the last forkful of cake, wiped her mouth, and headed back upstairs, leaving Cook shaking her head. This time Harriet went past the living room and continued up two more flights to her own bedroom. She took the phone into her room with her, sat down on her bed, and dialed Simon Rocque.

"Sport? Harriet here. Good news!"

Sport sighed. "No good news here," he told her. "School still pretty much sucks."

He had been telling her that every day since school had started. Harriet was concerned.

"Bugs and thullies still?" Harriet asked sympathetically. Sometimes it made a bad situation seem less bad if she switched beginning consonants. She had discovered this phenomenon when she was eight, and sick, and had heard her mother speaking on the phone to the pediatrician. "Domiting and viarrhea," her mother had said by mistake. It sounded so funny that Harriet had forgotten briefly to feel sick.

"Yeah, bugs and thullies," Sport said, and sighed again.

"Did you try what I suggested, taking chocolate-chip cookies to school as a bribe?"

"Yeah. It worked pretty well. I gave them out and everybody liked them okay. I doubled the walnuts."

"So?"

"Well, I can't do it every day. I have homework, and I have to clean the house—"

"Sport, your father got *married*. Doesn't *she* clean the house?"

Sport sighed. "Kate's not very good at it," he said. "She misses corners when she vacuums. I have to redo almost everything."

"I wonder why your dad married her." Harriet

herself could not cook very well, but she considered that a moot point as she wasn't certain she wanted to get married.

"She has many fine qualities," Sport said defensively. "And Harriet, that reminds me of something—"

"Wait. I have to tell you this. It's my good news! Ole Golly has taken action!"

"She's gone to the police? She turned herself in?" Sport sounded astonished.

"No, no, no. She'll never do that. She knows they'd beat a confession out of her even though she's innocent."

"What has she done, then?"

"She's going to a psychiatrist! To Morris Feigenbaum! She's seeking therapy!"

"Cool. She'll confess to him, I bet."

"Of course. But it will be *privileged*. He can never testify against her. But she'll be able to unburden herself. No more whimpering and muttering in her room. I'm so pleased for her, Sport. It's *good* to unburden oneself, don't you think?"

"Yeah."

Harriet waited, but he was silent.

"Sport? You seem distracted."

"I am."

"Why? You said you wanted to tell me something. What was it? Come on, Sport. Unburden yourself. And do it fast. I have to go someplace."

Harriet waited, but again there was a long silence on the other end of the line. She listened carefully.

"Sport," she said suddenly, "you're *blushing*, aren't you?"

"How can you tell?"

"You know I'm psychic. I can hear blushing." Harriet reached for her notebook. "Unburden yourself."

Sport sighed. "Remember the hairs?" he asked, still blushing.

"Of course."

"There are more," Sport said.

"Of course there are. They don't just stop coming."

"And something else," Sport mumbled.

Harriet opened her notebook and held her pencil poised. "Yes?" she said. "Continue."

"There's a girl in my school," Sport said with a groan. "She wears green shoes. And I think I'm in love."

"Oh my lord," Harriet said. "You're in for it now, Simon Rocque."

Five P.M. It was important to be precisely on time, Harriet felt. She rounded the corner and walked down the alley behind the Feigenbaums' house to the place where two large trash cans were placed behind a waist-high wooden barrier.

No one was there. She took out her notebook to make some notes about the meeting.

5 P.M. CAT IS STROLLING THROUGH YARD. I AWAIT ROSARITA SAUVAGE.

Harriet looked around. She said, "Hello, cat." The cat gave her a sidelong glance and continued its mysterious slow-motion errand through some weeds.

"Hi, H'spy!" Rosarita's voice was very loud, and Harriet jumped.

"Where are you?" she asked nervously.

"Close by, H'spy!"

Now Harriet identified the source of the voice. Angrily she pulled a tilted lid from one of the trash cans. Rosarita stood up.

"Here," Rosarita said. "I made two. One's for

you." She handed Harriet a long periscope created from cardboard tubes held together with shiny gray duct tape.

It was hard to stay angry with someone who was giving her a present. And the periscope was actually a pretty good gift. Harriet had made one in first grade, but this was a longer, more complex, more sophisticated periscope, and Harriet knew she would find it useful.

"Thank you. Is this how you were seeing me in my living room?"

"Yes. I was under your front steps using the Feigenbaums' cordless phone. Tip this can, would you? I had a heck of a time getting in. And now I can't get out."

Harriet helped Rosarita out of the trash can.

"I have to go back in a minute before they know I'm gone," Rosarita said, brushing dirt from her clothes. "I'm under surveillance all the time, but they get sloppy."

"Who's *they*? The Feigenbaums?"

Rosarita nodded.

"I know somebody who goes to Dr. Feigenbaum," Harriet told her. "Somebody who is very troubled."

"So what? Lots of people do. I hear them whining

and complaining in his office. Also they cry. I could even use my periscope and spy on them, but it would be too boring."

"Does he help them?" Harriet couldn't picture Ole Golly whining, but she did hope that the psychiatrist was going to be able to help her through her sadness.

"I guess." Rosarita shrugged.

Harriet changed the subject. "Did you start at your new school?"

"Yeah."

"How is it?"

"Same as my last school. Everybody hates me."

"Why?"

"Because I'm weird. And I'm flunking everything. I expect they'll kick me out."

Rosarita put her periscope to her eye and watched something in a nearby tree. "Squirrel," she said, and lowered the periscope. "Probably has rabies.

"I have to go in," she announced suddenly. "My jailers will freak if they realize I'm gone."

"Well, ah, thank you for the periscope. I really like it," Harriet said.

"It's junk," Rosarita said with a sneer.

"No, the interesting thing about it," Harriet explained, "is that you *made* it from junk, and it turned out to be something really, really useful. And also, it's always nice to get an unexpected gift. I'm probably going to make a note of it on my time line. I have this—"

But Rosarita had turned away. With a grand gesture she dropped her own periscope into the trash can. "Junk," she said loudly. Then she walked toward the back door of the Feigenbaums' house.

"Bye-bye, H'spy," she shouted. "Do call again."

CHAPTER 7

Harriet felt that Ole Golly should see Dr. Feigen-baum more often. She knew from observation that most of his patients had appointments once a week. But Ole Golly didn't. Almost a whole month passed after that first visit before she went to see him again.

Probably, Harriet realized, she couldn't afford more visits. Psychiatrists were very expensive. They didn't *do* much, either, for all that money, in Harriet's opinion. Last year when she had visited Dr. Wagner, Harriet had seen exactly what psychia-trists do: write in notebooks and play Monopoly. She loved the first but hated the second. And Dr.

Wagner had acted a little batty the whole time. It had been Harriet's first—and last—appointment with a psychiatrist

Since then she had spied on Morris Feigenbaum's office. She had actually stood briefly on tiptoe on the front stoop, balanced herself by holding onto the railing, and peered through the corner of the first-floor window. Then, when a passing taxi driver honked at her because he had nothing else to do and was a generally intrusive person, she had lost her balance and fallen into a small patch of pink impatiens surrounded by a fence. She had mashed some flowers, ripped her jeans, and skinned her knee, and had also had a very difficult and embarrassing time trying to climb over the fence and get out. It had not been one of her successful spying episodes.

But she *had* gotten a brief glimpse of Morris Feigenbaum at work with a patient. He sat there. He kept a notebook—similar to Harriet's—on his lap. Occasionally he wrote something. But mostly he just listened, and once in a while he blew his nose. The patient, a man sitting in another chair, was the one talking.

At least, that is what Harriet had observed

during the forty seconds she spent balanced and tee-tering before she fell into the pink impatiens. But she had also observed that his patients almost always looked happier on the way out than on the way in. She imagined they felt better after all that talking. And that intrigued her.

WHAT PSYCHIATRISTS DO

Harriet thought she might use this subject for a school report, so she kept the title in her notebook, but she had never figured out how to go beyond her opening thoughts. THEY TAKE ON YOUR BURDEN she had written tentatively. Then she had revised that to THEY HELP YOU LIFT YOUR BURDEN. And she believed it was true. It seemed you went to a psychiatrist if you felt burdened by something (grief and guilt and fear, in the case of Ole Golly), you told the psychiatrist about it, and then you were unburdened. Probably the psychiatrist was burdened then, but you didn't worry about that because you paid him to do it, and anyway, that's what he went to school for, so it wasn't as if he didn't know what he was getting into.

But Ole Golly seemed to be *more* troubled and

more burdened instead of less. So Harriet was puzzled. Harriet herself hadn't felt unburdened when she came out of Dr. Wagner's office—but she hadn't had anything to unburden. Ole Golly had a burden. Harriet was sure of it.

Also, Ole Golly had taken a small bag to each of her two visits to Dr. Feigenbaum, and Harriet was puzzled by that, too. It was not always the *same* bag; once it was simply plain brown paper, and the next time it was pale blue plastic. But it was a bag. Ole Golly went to her appointment carrying a bag and she returned home without it. She was taking *something* to Dr. Feigenbaum. If only Harriet had X-ray vision! If only she could see through the brown paper or the pale blue plastic and know what Ole Golly was taking across the street!

*   *   *

"What time is it there, *ma petite?*"

Harriet sighed. "Mother, it is always six hours earlier here than it is in Paris. It never changes. It is two P.M. here, Sunday afternoon. There's practically nothing on television but football."

"*Bien entendu.*"

"Please would you speak English? And also, is it

okay if I go to the downtown public library tomorrow after school? I need to do some research. I know how to get there on the subway. I never talk to strangers."

"Ask Miss Golly to take you," her mother suggested.

Harriet wrapped the telephone cord around her arm. It looked like an Egyptian bracelet, maybe an asp. "She takes a nap every afternoon. She hates it if I wake her up. I don't think she's feeling very well. You know she has problems," Harriet said meaningfully. After all, it was to her mother that Ole Golly had confided her innocence.

"Yes, she probably does need a nap," Harriet's mother said. "But Harriet, dear, see if a friend will go with you. I don't like you going that far alone on the subway."

"I'll ask Sport. If he says yes, can I go?"

"Yes. But don't linger. Don't dawdle. Don't—"

"I won't," Harriet promised. She unwound the asp and changed the subject.

.   .   .

"Ole Golly," Harriet said that night as she was getting ready for bed, "I'm going to the main library after school tomorrow. I asked Mother and she said it was all right. I called Sport and he said he'd go with me."

"Fine. Are you going to roll this up, Harriet, or will it be blocking the route to the bathroom all night?" Ole Golly was looking down at the time line, which had been increasing in length the more Harriet had been working on it. "It's just the width of a carpet. I might decide to walk on it if you leave it there."

"Don't you dare," Harriet said defensively, though she was fairly certain Ole Golly was joking. It was sometimes hard to tell because her face was always frowny. "You'd be stepping on your own name! See? You appear everywhere on this. You're the second most popular character on this time line. If there were Academy Awards for time lines, you'd be Best Supporting Actress." Harriet pointed to Ole Golly's name in several places.

Ole Golly leaned over to peer at it. "What does that say, at AGE THREE?" she asked.

Harriet read it to her in a fond voice. "FIRST HAIRCUT. OLE GOLLY SAVES SOME SNIPS OF HAIR."

"That's true," Ole Golly said. "I still have them. I gave some to your mother but she put them down on top of her dressing table, right beside some spilled powder. Later she wiped it all away. I kept mine, though, and put them into an album with your baby pictures."

"Did I have golden curls?" Harriet asked. "Like Beth Ellen Hansen?"

"Of course not. You had sensible hair. Beauty is skin deep, Harriet."

"I know," Harriet said, and sighed, thinking of Beth Ellen's curls with envy. Of course, spies would be hampered by great beauty because they would stand out in a crowd, which spies shouldn't do. But still.

"I remember that day," Ole Golly said. "You cried. You were frightened of the scissors." She touched Harriet's hair. "You need a haircut again, Harriet. You're unkempt." But she said it gently. Harriet could tell she wasn't really distressed.

"You took me everywhere," Harriet remembered. "For all my first things. My first party shoes. My first dentist's appointment. My first—"

"Well, let us not turn into a greeting card," Ole Golly said briskly. "The world has enough poor poetry and shallow sentiment. Roll it up now, and off to bed, Harriet. It's a school night."

Harriet unweighted the end of the time line and watched it roll itself up. "You took me to my very first day of school," she said. "I wore a blue dress." Harriet remembered crying a little bit that day. And it had been Ole Golly who had consoled her. Harriet had unburdened herself to Ole Golly on a number of occasions. Now it was Ole Golly who needed the unburdening.

"So you did. The dress was a little too large, but you grew into it."

"Every little girl in the world should have a you."

"Nonsense. Every child in the world should have adequate health care, access to education, strict but loving parents, and—" Ole Golly interrupted herself. "Enough of that. Good night, Harriet." She turned away abruptly, took a deep breath, stalked into her room, and closed the door.

* * *

"Sport," Harriet said, her shoulders slumping in frustration, "I'm not having any luck at all with this. I looked up *Waldenstein*, but everything I find is in German."

She and Sport were sitting side by side in the huge reading room at the New York Public Library.

"Hmmmm," Sport said. "I think that's a dead end. Let's try something else. Let's see if we can find something about his murder in a Canadian newspaper. Where did you say they lived?"

"Montreal."

"When would it have been, the murder?"

"Don't say *murder*. Say *death*. It was an accident. I know she's innocent."

"Death, then," Sport said.

Harriet thought. Ole Golly had arrived in mid-August. She had come by plane, and apparently the authorities had not been on the lookout for her at airports. So she had escaped quickly from Canada after accidentally expunging George Waldenstein. Probably there had been a proper funeral. Probably at first they had thought it a natural death, maybe from old age.

Even though Ole Golly refused to discuss age, Harriet knew from snooping and spying that she was forty-three. And George Waldenstein had been considerably older, at least fifty-five.

So probably his death could have seemed like an old-age one at first. Then somehow the Canadian Mounties had become suspicious. It wouldn't have taken them very long, even though they rode horses instead of driving cars. Then—although she was innocent—Ole Golly would have fled to New York.

"During the last week in July or the first week in August, I think," Harriet said, after visualizing the calendar and the events surrounding George Waldenstein's death.

"Okay, I'll go ask. You keep looking for Waldensteins while I'm gone."

Sport set out to put in his request at the reference desk. Harriet yawned and looked at the ceiling. She loved the New York Public Library reading room ceiling. It was covered in painted clouds. It made Harriet feel as if angels might at any moment begin to strum harps and hum songs in high, ringing voices. Harriet thought she might like to have clouds painted on the ceiling of her bedroom, but she was afraid that Brian Cleary, the painter who had applied fresh yellow paint to Ole Golly's room during the summer, would not know how to do clouds. Brian Cleary listened to baseball games on a small radio covered with paint spatters, and he swore a lot while he worked. If Ole Golly knew the bad language that Harriet had overheard coming from that room, she would probably not be willing to sleep in it.

Harriet waited a very long time for Sport. Finally he returned, carrying a bound stack of newspapers.

"Got it!" he said triumphantly. "*Montreal Gazette*! It's in English. They had some newspapers in French but I told them only English."

Together they leafed through the pages, reading obituaries.

But it was hopeless. It was as if George Walden-stein had never died, or even lived. Finally they closed up the *Montreal Gazettes* and left the library. Harriet wanted to stop in the gift shop. There were many things Harriet liked in the library gift shop, but the thing she liked best of all was a set of bronze bookends—reproductions of the two sculpted lions that guarded the front of the library. Harriet wanted the lion bookends very badly, and her birthday was coming up, so she thought it would be a good idea to stand in front of them and yearn. But Sport made her hurry past.

"You missed your cake and milk," Ole Golly said when Harriet arrived home.

"I know. I told you I was going to the library with Sport."

Harriet went into the upstairs study. She sat at her father's desk and began to write up the library trip in her notebook. Even though it had been an unsuccessful expedition, all spying events had to be documented. Later, when she was doing this as a career, she would have to send bills to clients. She knew they would demand to know how she had spent each hour, even fruitless hours like the trip to the library.

The telephone rang and Harriet answered. "Welsch residence."

"Simon Rocque here."

"You said you had to tend your leg of lamb and bake a pie."

"I do, but I forgot to ask you something."

Harriet closed her notebook. "So ask," she said, tilting her father's chair back so her feet lifted from the rug.

"This is not a question about Montreal, or spying," Sport explained.

"You're blushing again. It's about the girl with the green shoes, isn't it?" Harriet swiveled her father's desk chair so she was facing away from his desk, looking toward the bookcase. The telephone cord wrapped itself around her neck in a death grip.

"Sort of."

"Wait. I'm strangling." Harriet reversed her swivel and saved her own life.

"Okay," she said. "What's your question?"

"Well, do you think it would be okay if I invited her to my apartment after school, for pie?"

"How messy is it?"

"The pie? It's fine. It'll be messy when I put whipped cream on it, though."

"No, the apartment."

She waited and could feel Sport looking around. "It's okay," he said, "as long as I close the door to my dad's office. His office is always a mess." Matthew Rocque was the kind of writer who worked at home. Harriet had seen his office, and Sport was correct. His desk was piled with papers, and there were always several used coffee cups on the floor, sometimes with a plate or two bearing pieces of stale sandwich.

"I thought maybe when he got married, his wife—I mean your stepmother—would make him clean it up."

"No. Kate says she accepts that it's hopeless. And in return, he accepts that she hums country-and-western songs."

Harriet considered that. It seemed a fair trade. She thought about starting a page in her notebook with the heading COMPROMISES ONE MIGHT MAKE IN A MARRIAGE. Her parents had made compromises, she realized. Harriet's father didn't object if her mother spent a lot of money at Lord & Taylor. And Harriet's mother didn't object if her father sometimes was late for dinner.

"So what do you think, Harriet?"

Harriet tried to pay attention to Sport. "I guess it'd be okay. She'll have to ask her parents, though.

Be sure to tell her that your dad works at home. Most parents won't let a kid go to an apartment where there are no grown-ups."

"She doesn't have parents," Sport said.

"She's an *orphan?* Like the girl in *The Secret Garden?*"

"She's a refugee from a war-torn third-world country," Sport said in a solemn voice. "I heard her telling somebody."

"No kidding. So she'll have to ask a social worker or something. Maybe you ought to write the invitation formally, and have your father sign it, so it looks really legitimate. Put an RSVP."

"Good idea. Too late for this pie, though. It'd be stale by the time she RSVP'd."

"You can make another one. Try chocolate cream. You're good at those."

"Harriet." Sport spoke in a you're-trying-my-patience voice. "I'm good at *all* pies."

"Before you hang up," she said, "what's her name? I can't keep calling her just 'the girl with the green shoes.' "

Sport hesitated. Finally he said in a hushed and reverential tone, "Yolanda Montezuma."

CHAPTER 8

Harriet sighed and unrolled her time line. It was now a good three feet longer than it had been originally, as Harriet had been forced to tape on several more pages. Certain pivotal events simply could not go unrecorded. Its edges were a little frayed from all the rolling and unrolling. She had wanted it to remain crisp and neat, filled with fascinating reminders of her twelve years of life—well, twelve next week, just before Halloween—but it hadn't worked out that way. Some of the ink had smeared. There was a footprint on the entry of her poison ivy at age nine. And somehow a raisin had been smashed and stuck to the section marked EARLY CHILDHOOD SUCCESSES, where she had briefly noted her mastery of reading at age five, as well as her amazing ability—at three and four—to hold her breath for long periods of time, even though she had had an argument with Ole Golly about that notation.

"I'd hardly call that a success," Ole Golly had said, looking down at the breath-holding entry. "They were tantrums. You kicked your feet and held your breath until you turned blue. Your mother always wanted to call an ambulance, but I told her that it was simply a kind of manipulation."

"But remember you timed me in the bathtub? And I put my head underwater and stayed for an astounding length of time?"

"That was much later, Harriet. You were at least eight. You had fins and a snorkel."

When Harriet thought about it, she realized that Ole Golly was, not surprisingly, correct. She usually was. But the breath-holding notation was written in permanent marker—Ultra Fine Sharpie—so it couldn't be changed.

Carefully Harriet peeled the squashed raisin away and glared with distaste at the small stain it had left. She weighted the BIRTH end of the time line and crawled beside the length of the unrolled paper until she reached AGE TWELVE at the other end, which extended through the door of her bed-room into the hall. She lifted one leg of the telephone table and placed it on a corner of the paper to keep it flat. Then she stared at TWELFTH BIRTHDAY, wondering what events she might list, even though the birthday itself was still a week away.

Previous birthday notations included

SIXTH: CHICKEN POX; FIFTH: TRIP TO CIRCUS

with a subheading:

THREW UP ON FATHER'S TROUSERS (MIXTURE OF CRACKER JACK AND LEMONADE)

and

ELEVENTH: VISIT TO HARDWARE STORE WITH AUTHORIZED CHARGING PRIVILEGES (PURCHASE OF COMPLETE SET OF SPYING EQUIPMENT, INCLUDING BOY SCOUT KNIFE WITH SCREWDRIVER AND FLASHLIGHT WITH BLINKING AND FIL-TERING CAPACITY).

Recalling her eleventh birthday, just a year ago minus one week, Harriet smiled happily. Fondly she felt her tool belt—purchased on that birthday along with the spying tools, all of it on her father's charge account, and with his permission—and the loop that just fit the dangling flashlight, though it was not dangling there at the moment. Harriet kept the flashlight in the drawer of her bedside table when she didn't need it.

A shadow fell across her time line, and Harriet looked up at Ole Golly, who had come from her room across the hall and was looking down. As usual, she was swathed in tweed.

"Remember my parents gave you a beautiful blue silk dress for Christmas last year? Remember it has embroidery on the collar and the belt? You never wear it," Harriet pointed out.

"Silk is not intended for everyday wear," Ole Golly said with a sniff.

"Well, will you wear it for my birthday?"

"I think not."

For some reason Harriet wanted to poke Ole Golly, to jar her, to set her off-balance so she would turn back into the real Ole Golly instead of this mopey, disagreeable person she had become.

"I insist that you promise to wear your blue silk dress with the embroidered belt on my birthday," Harriet said.

"I think not."

"I humbly beg," Harriet said firmly. Humbly begging was something Harriet very rarely did. Ole Golly knew that she meant business when she humbly begged.

But Ole Golly's frowny face just turned frownier. "I will wear my blue silk dress next Easter," she replied after a moment.

Harriet had a sudden urge to rid Ole Golly's face of that frown. She felt she could lighten Ole Golly's spirits, ease her mind. If Dr. Feigenbaum wasn't helping her to unburden herself, maybe it was up to Harriet. Perhaps all Ole Golly needed was the opportunity to open up.

"Do you have a favorite birthday, Ole Golly?"

"Dostoievsky's is always nice. It's the day before Halloween."

"No, I mean one of your own. Maybe your thirtieth or fortieth or forty-third?" Harriet suggested, trying to steer Ole Golly toward her most recent birthday, the one she had shared with George Waldenstein.

"On my eighth birthday, my third-grade class went to the Metropolitan Museum of Art for a field trip. We saw a splendid exhibit on Matisse."

"Did you do anything special for your last birthday?"

Harriet felt that she was giving Ole Golly the opportunity to confess her great sadness at Mr. Waldenstein's sudden passing. To explain exactly why she sighed so, why she moped and stared all alone in her room. Harriet waited for the response.

"I celebrated in my usual manner. It was very nice, thank you," Ole Golly replied. And Harriet knew that was the end of that.

"Join me for tea? I was just going down to the kitchen," Ole Golly said.

Harriet looked at her watch. "And it's time for my cake and milk," she pointed out.

"Shall we descend, then?"

They did. Heading down the stairs behind Ole Golly, Harriet explained, "I was just thinking about my birthday coming up. Did you see that I had written TWELFTH BIRTHDAY on my time line?"

"I did. It made me think how quickly the years have gone." Ole Golly paused suddenly, on the step, and began to recite:

> "Backward, turn backward, O Time, in your flight!
>   Make me a child again, just for tonight!"

"Would you really want to be a child again?" Harriet asked.

Ole Golly sighed. "I suppose not," she said. "Roller-skating in Far Rockaway does not appeal. But turning time backward? Doing things differently, if one had the chance—"

At last, Harriet thought. She's going to unburden. The therapy has done it. At last we can have a talk about what went wrong in Montreal and why she accidentally killed Mr. Waldenstein, and maybe I can convince her to throw herself on the mercy of the Mounties. It is the flat-brimmed hats that make them look so stern; probably underneath they are kind and forgiving. And maybe she will be pardoned, because after all, she *is* innocent, and then she and I can resume our lives and the comfortable relationship we once had—

"What would you do differently, Ole Golly?" Harriet asked.

But Ole Golly didn't answer. She simply stood silently on the stairs. Harriet could tell she was thinking.

"I would have been much nicer to Pinky Whitehead in sixth grade," Harriet confessed. "He couldn't help it that he was thin, and dumb."

But Ole Golly didn't respond. She sighed, smoothed her tweed skirt absentmindedly, and looked into space.

"And, ah, I would have paid more attention in French class. My French is not as good as I'd like. What if I were to visit Montreal, and tried to—"

Harriet waited, hoping that mention of Montreal would trigger a response. And indeed, Ole Golly did seem to shake herself out of her private thoughts. She looked up, sniffed, and said, "Mmmm. Smell that, Harriet. I think she made a carrot cake. I believe I might go off my diet for an afternoon." She started down the stairs again.

"I didn't even know you were on a diet." Harriet followed her.

"Simply watching my weight, as all sensible people do."

"Mother's friend Sylvia Connelly goes off her diet on alternate Thursdays."

"I choose not to dignify that information with a response," Ole Golly said.

"Do you think Sylvia Connelly is an absolute stupe? I do." Harriet jumped the last remaining steps and followed Ole Golly into the kitchen just as the teakettle began to whistle. "And her sons, too. They talk dirty all the time behind her back, and she thinks they're such angels."

"Just a thin slice, please, Cook," Ole Golly said politely.

"Dirtily, I meant. They talk dirtily. It modifies *talk*, so it should be an adverb."

"A very thin slice," Ole Golly said, and Harriet knew she wasn't going to be lured into a conversation about the Connellys. Ole Golly refused to bad-mouth anybody, ever, even if they deserved it, and Harriet was quite certain that the Connelly twins did.

Cook poured the hot water from the teakettle into the teapot and set it on the table.

"Absolute stupes," Harriet repeated, just for her own amusement. "And I would not invite them to my birthday party, even if I were having a birthday party, which I am not. Cut me a huge wide piece, Cooky, would you? *I'm* not on a diet. I'm thin as a whippet, aren't I? Look." She held out her arm. "Whippet arms."

"Whippets do not have arms, Harriet," Ole Golly pointed out. She poured tea into two cups while Cook served the carrot cake and a glass of milk.

Harriet ignored her. She had no wish to discuss whippet body parts, not being entirely certain what a whippet *was*.

"I *love* your carrot cake, Cook!" Harriet poked her fork with enthusiasm into the thick slice on her plate.

Cook tasted it herself and got the look on her face, eyes half-closed, forehead furrowed, that meant she was assessing the success of the cake. Then she beamed, pleased with the taste. "I could make you one for your birthday, I suppose."

"I can't decide what to do for my birthday. I could go have a massage. I've always wanted to have a massage. Would you go with me, Ole Golly, and have a massage, too?"

"No," Ole Golly said, taking a small bite of cake.

"You know you have to be naked for a massage," Cook pointed out.

Harriet was astonished. "Isn't that illegal?"

Cook shrugged. "Not according to my niece. It cost her sixty dollars, too. If *I'm* going to be naked for somebody, they'd better pay *me* sixty dollars, that's all I got to say about that."

Harriet made a face. "Well, maybe I'll get a tattoo instead."

There was a silence. She looked up and saw that Cook and Ole Golly were both ignoring her very pointedly.

"Just a small one," Harriet said. "A tasteful one. Not a mermaid or anything."

They both looked at the ceiling. Cook hummed a little.

"Maybe a reproduction of Van Gogh's *Sun-flowers*."

But they still ignored her.

"Well, okay, maybe not. I don't know *what* I'll do. May I have some more cake, please?"

"Have your friends over for ice cream and cake. That's what people do on birthdays. They'll bring you presents, too," Cook said.

Harriet thought briefly about her friends at school. Janie Gibbs was her best school friend. She lived nearby. But Janie wasn't much fun at parties; she didn't like games and only wanted to talk about science experiments. Beth Ellen Hansen would probably bring an expensive present, because she was very rich, but she didn't understand the kind of gifts Harriet liked, and she would undoubtedly bring some frilly nonunisex clothing, the last thing Harriet wanted for her birthday.

Then there were Rachel, Marion, Carrie, and Laura. They had once stolen Harriet's notebook, for which Harriet would never completely forgive them. Still, they were her friends, and they had invited Harriet to *their* parties over the years. But when Harriet thought about a party filled with seventh-grade girls, she pictured a lot of giggling and gossip, just like what she listened to, bored out of her mind, every day at school lunch. She wished she knew someone unusual and fascinating. Someone mysterious, perhaps, with dark secrets yet to be disclosed. She wished she could invite—

"Rosarita Sauvage!"

Cook and Ole Golly looked startled.

"She's a girl I met! I bet she's a lot more interesting than any girl from my school! I could invite her!"

"Does she like carrot cake?" Cook asked.

"Of course. Everyone does. And also Yolanda Montezuma!"

"Who is that?" asked Ole Golly.

"A girl Sport has a crush on. She goes to his school. He's hardly ever talked to her, only worshipped her from afar. But this could be a breakthrough for him. Of course, I'll invite Sport, too."

"What kind of people are those?" Cook muttered. "I never heard such strange names in my whole life, did you, Miss Golly?"

Ole Golly smashed her last cake crumbs neatly with the back of her fork and ate them. "Actually," she said, "I know a girl, the niece of a friend of mine, just Harriet's age or thereabouts, who has an equally odd name."

"What is it?" Harriet asked. She could hardly believe there was another name as unusual.

Ole Golly shook her head in amusement. "Zoe Carpaccio," she said. "Or so she tells me."

That did it. "Invite her," Harriet commanded. "I'm going right upstairs to make invitations."

* * *

But no one could come. No one but Sport. One after another, they declined.

Rosarita Sauvage telephoned after Harriet slipped an invitation into the mail slot of the Feigenbaums' house on her way home from school.

"H'spy?"

"Yes. Did you get my invitation?"

"Don't cry, H'spy, but parties are forbidden by my religion," Rosarita said in a haughty voice.

Harriet had opened her notebook to the page marked with Rosarita's name. She hoped to find out some facts about the mysterious girl.

"What *is* your religion?" she asked politely.

"Exclusionist."

Harriet wrote it down, guessing at the spelling. "What do people with that religion do on their birthdays?" she asked.

"We don't believe in birthdays," Rosarita replied impatiently.

"But—"

"I have to go shave my head now. G'bye, H'spy." Rosarita Sauvage hung up.

"You're really *rude*, you know that?" Harriet said loudly, but she was talking to a dial tone.

Harriet drew an oval in the notebook, like a head with no hair. She made an N in front of it, turning it into the word NO. She was sitting there staring at it when Ole Golly came up the stairs, looking solemn.

"Harriet, I'm sorry to tell you this, but my friend's niece—"

"Oh yes, Zoe Carpaccio." Harriet flipped a page in her notebook and found the place where she had written that name. "Don't tell me she has to shave her head."

"Why would I tell you that?" Ole Golly asked. "She has lovely hair. But unfortunately she can't come to your birthday party."

Harriet wrote NO on the page under Zoe Carpaccio's name. "Why not?" she asked.

"My friend called while you were at school and said that her niece has other plans that afternoon. She didn't say what."

"That's impolite, not to say what."

"Well, let us not dwell on it."

Harriet scowled and closed her notebook. The telephone rang. "That'll be Sport," Harriet predicted angrily, reaching for the phone, "saying that Yolanda Montezuma can't come, either."

It was exactly that.

"What excuse did *she* give?" Harriet asked Sport.

"None."

"*None?*"

"Well, I didn't really give her a chance. It was the first time I ever approached her, Harriet, and I was very nervous and blushy. So I just went up to her in the hall at school, handed her the invitation, and stood there waiting while she read it. Then she said, 'Tell her no,' and I didn't wait around to hear the reason."

"You have no social skills, Sport," Harriet told him. "None at all."

"I know. I'm a total loser." Poor Sport, she thought. He sounded pathetic.

Harriet opened her notebook to Yolanda Montezuma's page and wrote NO below the name. She felt defeated.

"I feel defeated," she said to Sport. "I guess I'll

just go visit the homeless on my birthday. Maybe I'll distribute carrot cake."

"I do have some other news, though," Sport said. He had lowered his voice.

"Speak up. What other news? Good or bad?"

"I'm not sure. Good, I think. Is Ole Golly around?"

"No. She was here, but she went in her room and closed the door. Why?"

"I don't want her to hear about this."

"Should I write it in my notebook?" Harriet found that she had lowered her voice now, too.

"Yes," Sport whispered. "Turn to the George Waldenstein section."

"Wait. That's in my Ole Golly section." There were several pages, actually, devoted to Mr. Waldenstein; the entries dated back to the days when he had courted Ole Golly, riding his deliveryman's bike to East Eighty-seventh to have tea in the kitchen or to take Ole Golly, perched behind him, to the movies.

Harriet remembered one particular evening. The courtship had been new then, and Harriet had stayed awake and spied from her bedroom window to check on the kissing part.

There were several pages devoted to the romance between Catherine Golly and George Waldenstein. Finally one page simply had three phrases:

MARRIAGE.
MOVE TO MONTREAL.
FAREWELL, OLE GOLLY.

Tucked between the pages was the goodbye letter Ole Golly had written to Harriet. It still made her feel a little choked up to read it.

"Are you there, Harriet?"

Harriet looked at the final page, on which quite recently she had written meticulously with a wide-tipped pen:

REST IN PEACE, GEORGE WALDENSTEIN.

She read the final notation to Sport. "I feel that I should add 'Ole Golly is innocent,' " she said, "but I don't want to ruin the way it looks."

"Harriet, here's the news. Guess what?"

"What?"

"George Waldenstein is alive. I just talked to him."

CHAPTER 9

"What do you mean? How can that be?"

"Well, I kept thinking about it and thinking about it," Sport explained, "and even though *you're* the spying expert, Harriet, I thought maybe you had overlooked something. It occurred to me—"

"I never overlook anything. Did you just call to insult me, Simon Rocque? Because I have other things I could be doing. I have plenty of homework: a book report to write, and a chapter of history to read. Or I could be visiting the homeless right now."

"No, I'm sorry, Harriet. Listen. I called the Vital Statistics Office in Montreal, and—no Waldenstein death."

Harriet looked at her elaborate

and hoped that she would not have to erase it. It was the best lettering she had ever done.

"So then," Sport went on, "I called the Royal Canadian Mounted Police—the Mounties—but they had no information about the murder of a George Waldenstein or the flight of his wife."

"The *flight?*"

"You know what I mean. The fleeing."

"Get to the point, Sport."

"Well, by then it was pretty clear that there hadn't been a murder. So I just called Montreal directory assistance and asked for George Waldenstein's phone number. I thought maybe someone would still be there; maybe some relative who could give me the details about his death. I was going to pretend to be a long-lost cousin. And then I *called* it, Harriet. My father is going to kill me when the phone bill comes. But I called the number, and he answered. 'George Waldenstein,' he said. Not even 'Hello.' Just 'George Waldenstein.' "

"Did he sound healthy?"

"I guess so. I got flustered. I pretended I had a wrong number, and I hung up."

"Wait. Shhh." Ole Golly's door had opened.

Harriet looked up at her with a cheerful smile. "I'm just talking to Sport," she said.

Ole Golly adjusted her sleeves. She was wearing her usual layers of tweed—her things, as she called them—with a tweed shawl draped over everything. "I have an appointment," she said. "I'll be back in time to have a snack with you."

"Okay, bye." Harriet watched as Ole Golly went back into her room and picked up her purse and a small gift bag from Saks, the size that would hold a bottle of perfume. Then she headed down the stairs. Harriet waited, listening, and heard the front door close. Then she adjusted her glasses, tucked her hair behind her ear, and resumed her phone conversation.

"Sport? Are you still there?"

"Yes, but I wouldn't have waited much longer, Harriet. I have a casserole to make."

"Sorry. It was Ole Golly. She went out. And Sport, I watched her as she went down the stairs. She was carrying a small bag again. She goes out with a small bag, and she comes home without it, every time. She's *delivering* something."

"Making a drop. That's what they call it."

"Who calls it that?"

"Drug dealers," Sport said. "She could have brought something down from Canada. They wouldn't stop her at the border because of the way she looks."

"That is absolutely absurd."

"Harriet, even Ole Golly was once a very impressionable and rebellious adolescent. She might have gotten hooked on something back then while she searched for her identity in inappropriate and self-destructive ways."

"Are you reading from a pamphlet?"

"Yes," Sport confessed. "It's here on my father's desk. He's researching an article about the lost dreams of urban youth."

"Ole Golly was never an urban youth. She grew up in Far Rockaway. She roller-skated all the time. Her favorite book was *A Girl of the Limberlost.*"

"Follow her to the drop," Sport said. "It might not be too late to extricate her."

"Wait a minute. Hang on, Sport. Let me go look out the window."

In a moment Harriet was back. "As I guessed," she said. "She was only going across the street to her psychiatrist. I just watched her enter Dr. Feigenbaum's front door."

"You don't take a bag of cocaine to a psychiatrist."

"You certainly don't," Harriet agreed. "I think you'd better stick to your dream of becoming a chef. You're not cut out to be a spy, Sport."

"Call me back, Harriet. I really have to put this casserole together."

"Ten-four. Over and out," Harriet said.

●　●　●

Ten minutes later, Harriet was in the yard behind the Feigenbaums' brownstone, peering through her binoculars. She did not see Ole Golly. Dr. Morris Feigenbaum's office was in the front of the house to the left of the stairs, but Harriet thought there was a possibility that drug dealers might be lurking in the backyard, waiting for the goods to be delivered. She had brought her heavy flashlight along, dangling from its special loop on her belt, even though it was daylight. If she needed to bash a drug dealer over the head, she would use the flashlight as a weapon.

But there was no one in the yard except, once again, a cat.

And once again Rosarita Sauvage came to the back door and called, "Here, kitty." Today her hair was tied in two ponytails.

Harriet put down the binoculars and glared at her angrily.

"You're a stupe and a liar!" she called.

The girl squinted her eyes and glared back at Harriet. "Why, H'spy?"

"You said you were shaving your head!"

Rosarita shrugged. "This is a wig," she said. Then she picked up the cat, turned, and went back into the house, smoothing the cat's fur and talking to it in a high, babyish voice.

IN NO WAY IS ROSARITA SAUVAGE WEARING A WIG. I CAN ALWAYS TELL WIGS. SYLVIA CONNELLY WEARS WIGS. THEY HAVE A LINE AROUND THE EDGE WITH NO JIBBERY PARTS OR LITTLE HAIRS. ROSARITA IS A LIAR AND A FINK AND HAS HAIR AND I AM VERY GLAD SHE COULD NOT COME TO MY BIRTHDAY.

Harriet snapped her notebook closed and replaced it in her pocket. With a hand on her weapon-flashlight, she made one more survey of the yard and the alley, checking for drug dealers. Nothing. *Rien*, as Ole Golly would say in French.

She could feel her shoulders lower into a slump. If Ole Golly were nearby, Harriet knew, she would glare and mutter sharply, "Posture."

But Ole Golly had disappeared into the office of the psychiatrist/drug dealer, grasping her Saks bag of who-knew-what, and Harriet stood alone in an alley with her spy tools and her slumped shoulders, feeling like a failure and a stupe, and not yet even twelve years old.

She decided to go to church.

* * *

There were many churches in Harriet's section of Manhattan. She had tried most of the churches at various times, dropping in on weddings on Saturday afternoons, usually in the spring and summer, when most weddings seemed to be held, and occasionally checking out the rummage sales and craft fairs toward Christmas.

She had decided that she liked the Catholic churches best. They had mournful statues, nothing overly cheerful-looking. Harriet was a little suspicious of churches where colorful banners appliquéd with flowers and multiracial children hung on the walls. She had nothing against either flowers or children; she just didn't think they should be flapping from the walls of churches. It wasn't solemn enough.

Once, she had wandered into an Episcopal church on a Saturday afternoon, hoping for a wedding—Episcopal weddings were usually pretty good, with many bridesmaids—but instead of a wedding, there had been a string quartet performing. Three men in dark suits and a woman in a long black dress were up at the front of the church with violins, a cello, and a viola. They were industriously playing a very long piece of music. Every now and then they stopped but then they would start again. No one clapped. One gray-haired man in a back pew was sound asleep.

Later she happened into the same church, also on a Saturday afternoon, and found, instead of the string players in their serious black clothes, a group of jazz musicians—one had a pierced nostril, Harriet could see—playing very raucous music and wearing unserious clothing. The people in the pews didn't seem to mind. They were tapping their toes. Harriet sat down and listened for a while, but when the saxophone player put down his instrument and began to sing a song about *"Oooh, oooh, oooh, what a little moonlight can do . . . ooo . . . ooo,"* she felt shocked and worried, as if the saints in the stained-glass windows might begin to mutter and grumble. So she left.

Now, except for weddings, Harriet only dropped in on Catholic churches. There were many in her vicinity. She liked their names, especially the ones that began with *Our Lady*. Our Lady of Peace was on East Sixty-second Street and Our Lady of Perpetual Help on East Sixty-first. Harriet envisioned the ladies dropping by for coffee with one another, and maybe discussing the price of candles and the sad state of the homeless.

Perpetual help was what Harriet felt she needed, but the Perpetual Help lady was quite a long walk, and it was almost time for her snack. She knew that Ole Golly would be headed home from the Feigenbaums' and would wonder where she was. So she visited, instead of a Lady, the nearby St. Joseph's.

No one was home, but the door was unlocked and Harriet let herself inside the dimly lit sanctuary. She decided to light a candle, which was something even non-Catholics like Harriet were allowed to do. She had done it often, sometimes even with priests and nuns watching, and no one had ever frowned or shook a head or a finger at her in a scolding way. She always put some money into the box first.

Today she also carefully removed her belt of

spy tools and laid it on a cushioned seat. It seemed inappropriate to light a Catholic candle while wearing a knife—even if it was only a Boy Scout knife.

Harriet deposited her money, eighty cents that she found in the pocket of her jacket, and carefully lit one small candle at the end of the row. The others flickered. Then Harriet knelt. She felt it was the thing to do.

Respectfully she said in a soft voice, "Ah, hello, God. I am looking for perpetual help but I didn't have time to go all the way down to Sixty-first Street, even by subway or bus.

"I'm not a Catholic, I want to be honest with you about that," Harriet added, "but I did put money in the box. Eighty cents."

She waited a moment, on her knees, watching the candlelight, trying to decide how to begin.

"It's hard to explain, but, well, I have this friend who is innocent of something. I am not certain what, exactly." She spoke quickly because she didn't know how much time she was allowed for eighty cents. Then she waited, listening, glancing up toward the high ceiling, hoping that somehow an answer would come.

"I would ask you to forgive her because I know that's what you're there for. But she's innocent, I'm sure of it. She only *feels* guilty. And maybe she's being manipulated by evil people. You've probably heard that before." Harriet sighed, wondering what additional information she could provide to God.

Then she remembered something. "As long as I'm here," she began, "I'll tell you who you *can* forgive. Three people. Rosarita Sauvage, for one. Yolanda Montezuma. And Zoe Carpaccio. Every single one of them refused to come to my birthday party, God, and without good reason. Please forgive them for that."

Her knees were starting to hurt. Also, she had begun to feel a little angry. "And listen, God? Would you also please punish them? Severely? I know it's part of your job.

"And while I'm here," Harriet added, "I'll just mention that I would like lion bookends for my birthday next week.

"Ten-four. Amen. Goodbye." She waited for a moment, thinking, and then added, "RSVP." Then she stood up. She looked at her watch. It was time for her cake and milk.

Harriet retrieved her spy belt from the pew where she had left it. Carefully she rebuckled it so that the notebook and flashlight were at the back—it was uncomfortable when they dangled in the front; they bumped her thighs. She turned to leave. At the door she stopped, looked up, and confided politely, "That last part was French," just in case God was not bilingual. "It means *Please reply*."

Then Harriet left the church and headed home.

CHAPTER 10

God did not RSVP. Harriet waited three weeks but heard nothing. *Rude*, she thought.

Her birthday passed without a party. Her parents sent a check but it was not enough for the lion bookends, which cost $150. Cook gave her a gold-plated heart-shaped locket with a large red stone in the center, which Harriet wore for two days to be polite. At school her friends sang to her in the lunchroom, and Sport sent her a card with a cartoon of penguins on an iceberg, and inside, a bad but rhyming verse about the warmth of friendship.

Ole Golly gave her a volume of Emily Dickinson poems, and Harriet thought it was the best birthday gift she had received. It almost made up for no party and no lion bookends.

"Listen!" Harriet said to Ole Golly. "The punctuation is all funny but I can tell just what she means!" She opened the book and read:

The Red—Blaze—is the Morning—
The Violet—is Noon—
The Yellow—Day—is falling—
And after that—is none—

"That was Poem Four Sixty-nine," Harriet said. "They all have numbers! Pick a number, Ole Golly. There are zillions."

Ole Golly thought for a moment and then chose. "Six Thirty-one," she said.

Harriet found it and began to read:

Ourselves were wed one summer—dear—

She stopped abruptly when she saw Ole Golly's face. Six hundred thirty-one had been a bad choice.

"That wasn't a very good one," Harriet said, flustered. "Probably even Emily Dickinson had some bad writing days. But I really, really love the book, Ole Golly."

* * *

Harriet started a new section in her notebook. She did it reluctantly because she had only a few blank pages left, and she wasn't entirely certain she wanted to use any of the remaining ones on religion. But she did have religious questions, and the best way to ponder questions, she had found over the years, was to do so in her notebook. So she turned to a blank page and wrote:

RELIGION

WHAT IS THE POINT OF RELIGION EXACTLY IF GOD DOES NOT ANSWER YOUR REQUESTS, OR EVEN RÉPONDEZ S'IL VOUS PLAÎT, EVEN IF YOU SPEND ALL YOUR MONEY ON CANDLES AND MAKE YOUR REQUESTS KNEELING AND WITH A WHOLE LOT OF COURTESY?

After she had written that, Harriet tried very hard to remember if she had said *please* during her moments in the church. She usually did. Her parents, her teachers, and Ole Golly all thought of Harriet as a highly courteous person.

Still, her request had not been granted. She had checked. And Harriet felt sure she had been courteous to God.

"How is Yolanda Montezuma?" she asked Sport later. "Has she had any serious troubles lately, as if a punishment of some sort had been inflicted upon her?" She thought for a moment about possible Godlike biblical language and added, "Or meted? Does it appear that someone has meted out a punishment?"

Sport shook his head. "She looks okay," he said. "She never talks to me. I can't even figure out why I'm in love with her. She's only talked to me twice."

"Only twice?"

"The first time was in the hall at school. That's how we met. I dropped all my books, and I was picking them up when I saw these green shoes stop beside me. She helped me pick up a pencil that had rolled away."

"You met over a rolled pencil? It sounds like a movie meeting. The hero and heroine have this situation that throws them together and suddenly their eyes meet, and that's it. Love. I've seen lots of movies like that, Sport."

"I know. Usually it's in a bookstore or a library. Sometimes their eyes meet through a gap in a bookcase."

"Did your eyes meet like that?"

Sport thought about it. It was a Saturday afternoon in November, and he and Harriet were walking along Eighty-seventh Street on their way from her house to his apartment.

"Well, our eyes sort of met," he said. "She handed me the pencil, and I fell in love, just like that—ZAP—so I said, 'I'm Simon Rocque.' I guess, actually, I said thank you first. *Then* I said 'I'm Simon Rocque.' "

"And you were already in love? It happened that fast?"

"Yes. Like a car, from zero to sixty. Zap."

"And then what happened?"

"Ah, let me think. She stared at me for a minute. Then she said, 'Yolanda Montezuma.' That was it."

"You said you talked to her twice, though."

"Well, the next time was when I gave her the party invitation, Harriet. I said, 'Here.' Then I stood there waiting while she read it, and then she said, 'Tell her no.' "

Harriet had counted. "So in your entire relationship, Sport, you have said six words to her, and she has said five words to you."

Sport nodded.

"And you love her still."

He looked embarrassed and nodded again.

"You're pitiful, Sport. And she deserves punishment. I can't figure out why God doesn't see that. Cook says God is all-knowing, but as far as I can tell, God hasn't punished Rosarita Sauvage yet, either. *They* are the reason I didn't have a birthday party, Sport. They, and someone else named Zoe Carpaccio, who *also* remains unpunished, according to Ole Golly."

"I would've come."

"You *did* come, Sport. Remember, it was you and me and Cook and Ole Golly. It wasn't a party exactly, but at least we had cake."

"If I'd known it was a party, I would've brought a present, Harriet."

"The only thing I can think of that I want," Harriet told Sport, "is for Ole Golly to be the way she used to be."

"She was always pretty grouchy," Sport pointed out.

"Yes, but she was full of wisdom and she was very strong in her opinions. I think she was psychologically sound. But now—"

"Now what?" They had reached the Rocques' building.

"Now she sighs and mutters and carries a little bag around all the time," Harriet said. "She spends a lot of her time closed in her room. She takes naps.

She says she's unwell. And she doesn't pay very much attention to me at all."

At just that moment Harriet got a glimpse, just a glimpse, of a very familiar-looking tall woman enveloped in bulky tweed. She was on the next block, just turning a corner.

"Sport! Look!"

"Where?"

"I saw Ole Golly! We've got to follow her!" Harriet pointed to the corner and headed off at a brisk jog. "Stay close," she said to Sport, "and try to be invisible. *Blend*."

"Blend?"

"Into the woodwork. Especially now, as we turn the corner. We can't let her see us."

Carefully they edged around the corner of a small hosiery shop with a lot of fake legs wearing brightly striped tights in the window. Harriet peered toward the next block and got a glimpse of the familiar tweeds. Ole Golly was walking purposefully, as if she had a destination in mind but was not in a hurry.

Fortunately, on a Saturday, there were large numbers of people out and about in the neighborhood, and it was easy for Harriet and Sport to make themselves invisible. They ducked into a doorway for a moment when Ole Golly stopped briefly, entered a convenience store, and emerged with a magazine under her arm.

"What did she buy?" Harriet whispered to Sport. "Can you see? I think I need new glasses."

Leaning from the doorway, Sport squinted at the magazine.

"Literary?" Harriet asked. "Or news, maybe?"

"I can't get the title," Sport said, "but it has a movie star on the cover."

"No!" Harriet was shocked. "That's completely out of character!" she said. "She's having a breakdown, Sport. She disdains trashy magazines. She reads them only in waiting rooms."

"Maybe she's going to the dentist," Sport suggested.

Harriet shook her head. "She goes to Dr. Van Pelt. His office is on the other side of town."

"Maybe she bought it for someone else."

"No, she'd never do that. We went to tea once at Sylvia Connelly's and later Ole Golly told me she was shocked to see a *Cosmopolitan* in the bathroom. Walk faster, Sport; we might lose her."

Sport sped up and they continued to trail Ole Golly.

"Look!" Harriet whispered as they approached

the corner of Eighty-sixth Street and Lexington Avenue. "She's going to take the subway someplace! Do you have any money? I don't."

"Look! She's changed her mind!"

It was true. Ole Golly had started toward the subway entrance. Then, after pausing for a moment, she seemed to make a decision. She stepped to the edge of the curb and looked down the street. She raised one arm as a signal.

"She's taking a cab instead! Hurry, Sport! Get closer and see if you can hear what she tells the cab driver. I'll lurk here so she doesn't see me."

With his head down, Sport made his way quickly toward the corner where Ole Golly was standing. She didn't look his way. He walked beside a man in a dark green jacket as if he were with the man, as if they were perhaps father and son.

Good work, Sport, Harriet thought, watching him. Good spying maneuver!

No bag, Harriet noticed. Today Ole Golly was not carrying anything but her purse and the magazine she had just bought.

Sport stood on the corner as people waited for the light to change. He was very close to Ole Golly when a Yellow Cab pulled up and she got into it. When the cab pulled away as the light changed to green, Sport scurried back to where Harriet was waiting.

"What did you hear?" she asked eagerly. "Where is she going?"

"East Sixty-eighth, something something something something."

"What do you mean, something something something something?"

"I couldn't hear what she said after East Sixty-eighth. It was a lot of syllables."

Harriet sighed. "Well, it's a start. East Sixty-eighth. And we're standing on East Eighty-sixth. Eighteen blocks. There's a lot of traffic. Her cab might hit a lot of red lights. We might catch up with her if we walk fast."

Harriet started off. After a moment Sport sighed and ran to catch up with her. "Harriet," he said, "it'll be *thirty-six* blocks, because we'll have to turn around and come back."

"Eighteen plus eighteen. You're right." Harriet strode forward. "Hurry, we're losing her."

CHAPTER 11

"COUNCIL ON FOREIGN RELATIONS," Sport read aloud, standing in front of the building. "That's gotta be it. That's where she was headed," he said.

They had lost sight of the cab carrying Ole Golly as they hurried down block after block. Now here they were, at her destination street—East Sixty-eighth—after their eighteen-block rush, but they had no idea where she was or which building she might have entered.

"Really," Sport said. "That really could be it."

Harriet stared at the sign and tried to figure out why Sport felt this was it. Carefully she wrote COUN-CIL ON FOREIGN RELATIONS in her notebook. She had started a page with the heading EAST 68TH STREET.

"Why?" she asked Sport finally. "Why does that have to be it?"

"Because she *has* some foreign relations! She has George Waldenstein up there in Canada."

It didn't sound right to Harriet, though she wasn't exactly certain why. "I don't think that's what it means, Sport," she said finally, and turned away from the building. "I really don't think she's in there. But I'll check.

"Excuse me?" Harriet approached a man who was leaning against a post smoking a cigarette. He raised an eyebrow at her.

"Have you been here long?"

The man nodded. He pointed toward his own feet, to show her the remains of three crushed cigarettes on the sidewalk.

"Did you see a tall woman with a frowny face wearing tweed things go into this foreign relations building?

"I'm an investigator," Harriet added, in case he thought she was simply a nosy person. A lot of people thought that about Harriet.

The man seemed to mull it over for a moment. "No," he said finally. "A guy delivering a pizza went in. And then he came out. That's all."

"Thank you," Harriet said politely. "Come on, Sport. She must have gone someplace else on Sixty-eighth. Let's see what else there is."

"My feet can't take any more." Sport stopped a few steps later and pointed at a building. "How about this?"

"INDONESIAN CONSULATE," Harriet read. "Could she be planning to run away to Indonesia?"

"You can't run there. You have to fly. It's halfway around the world," Sport pointed out. "I think it's next to China."

"Ole Golly doesn't like Chinese food. She says it has too many mysterious ingredients. I doubt if she'd go there." Harriet wrote it down in her notebook anyway as she walked by.

"CENTER FOR AFRICAN ART," Sport read aloud. "I wonder if they have a bathroom."

"Sport! Don't tell me you have to—"

"I have to."

Guys, thought Harriet impatiently. Guys always went to the bathroom more often than girls. There was probably a physiological reason, Harriet suspected, but she hadn't done any research. Maybe it could be her seventh-grade science project in the spring.

When Sport finally emerged, looking more comfortable, they resumed their search.

"Okay, you do one side and I'll do the other. That way it will only take half as long."

They separated and each trudged down one side of the block. Then they met at the next corner to compare findings.

Harriet carefully wrote down the names of all of the buildings on Sixty-eighth Street in her notebook. She underlined them.

"This has to be it, Sport," she said once they had gone through the list. "It wasn't Indonesia, and it wasn't the Center for African Art, and it wasn't Judaica Silver."

"Or the Hellenic Medical Society," Sport reminded her.

"And there's nothing else except the hospital buildings farther up. This must be it. It makes sense."

Together they looked solemnly at the information in Harriet's notebook.

DIVORCE MEDIATORS

and

CONFIDENTIAL SEARCH, INC., EMPLOYMENT AGENCY

"First she gets herself divorced from George Waldenstein," Harriet said. "Then she gets a job."

"But, Harriet," Sport pointed out, "she already *has* a job. She works for your parents. She takes care of you."

"I'm twelve years and two weeks old, Sport," Harriet pointed out. "Look at me. I'm on East Sixty-eighth Street. I walked here. I don't *need* taking care of anymore.

"Last year, after she left to go to Montreal, Ole Golly wrote me a letter. I memorized it."

Sport was listening.

"I'm not going to tell you the intimate parts," Harriet explained. "But it ended this way: '*You don't need me now. You're eleven years old, which is old enough to get busy at growing up to be the person you want to be.*'"

Harriet and Sport stood silently for a moment.

"What is the person you want to be, Harriet?" Sport asked.

"Spy. Writer. Philanthropist. That's all I've decided so far. How about you?"

"Chef, and I don't know what else," Sport said. He looked down at his tired feet. "I guess I can eliminate toe dancer, though," he added glumly.

They turned, crossed the street, and began walking north. They didn't talk at all.

Then, suddenly, as they waited for the light to change so they could cross Seventy-ninth Street, Harriet turned to Sport. "It's true, what Ole Golly said," she told him. "I don't need her now. But you know what?"

"What?"

"She needs me. I'm sure of it. She needs me for *something*, but I don't know what. I can't ask her. I actually tried to talk to her about the fact that she's changed, but she just gets even more frowny. She tells me to leave her room. I've left her room when she's asked, but I won't leave the mystery of what she needs me for unsolved."

◦ ◦ ◦

That night Harriet, in her pajamas, unrolled her time line and inserted as a major entry under AGE TWELVE:

BEGINS TO CONSIDER NEW YORK MARATHON

"What's that all about?" asked Ole Golly, peering down at it dubiously.

"Well, I'm just considering it. I haven't committed myself. But I walked a whole lot today. I think I might be in pretty good shape. Sport's father ran in the marathon once, and he got his picture on TV."

" '*Fools' names, like fools' faces—*' " Ole Golly replied.

"I know," Harriet said, and finished the quotation—" '*are often seen in public places.*' "

"Indeed," Ole Golly said with a sniff, and returned to her room. For a moment she had seemed almost her old self, peering and quoting and sniffing. But Harriet wasn't deceived. She'd noticed recently, for one thing, that Ole Golly was walking very slowly, with her shoulders slumped. This was not at all in character; Ole Golly had *always* been a posture nut, a champion of straight shoulders and brisk step—and also, the peering and sniffing had been halfhearted. Ole Golly wasn't *really* interested in Harriet's thoughts about the marathon. She was simply going through the motions. Her mind and her heart were clearly someplace else.

But where? In Montreal with George Waldenstein, who was still alive, according to Sport, but whom Ole Golly absolutely refused to discuss?

Or were her thoughts on East Sixty-eighth Street, which Harriet now knew was an extremely meaningful site?

For a moment Harriet thought about approaching Ole Golly's closed door. She looked down at her feet, which were bare and clean, just out of the bathtub. Harriet liked her feet. They were sturdy and symmetrical, and they had just walked her thirty-six blocks without complaining, unlike Sport's much more pitiful feet, which Harriet had once noticed had oddly shaped big toes.

Harriet tried to command her feet through telepathy to stand and walk firmly to Ole Golly's door. She tried to order her right hand to make a fist and thump loudly on the door. She tried to command her voice to say in a forthright, forceful way, "Ole Golly, the time has come. We must talk. I demand to know what is happening!"

But her body did not respond. Her clean pink feet did not stand. Her right hand simply continued to hold the pen with which she had been writing on the time line. And her voice, instead of barking out a forceful statement, simply got swallowed up in a timid, uncertain little cough.

What kind of spy am I, anyway? Harriet asked herself in despair. A decent, self-respecting spy would be able to make her feet march across to that door.

But she knew that a loud, demanding thump on

that door followed by a forthright, demanding question would cause Ole Golly pain. Not that Ole Golly would ever, ever admit it. No. She would be stoic and sensible, Harriet knew, and she would likely send Harriet off to bed in a firm and slightly scolding voice with a reminder to hang up the damp towel draped over the toilet seat.

But she would be hurt and disappointed and her privacy would be invaded if Harriet thumped on that door. It was not the appropriate course of action, even for the most stalwart spy. So Harriet sighed and thought things through as she rolled up her time line for the night.

Seated on her bed, Harriet opened her notebook and began to make a list of clues.

1. OLE GOLLY LEFT GEORGE WALDENSTEIN (WHO IS ALIVE) AND CAME TO NEW YORK.

2. SHE IS SAD AND DEPRESSED AND GROUCHY AND UN-WELL.

3. SHE STARTED GOING REGULARLY TO DR. FEIGENBAUM.

4. SHE TAKES SOMETHING TO DR. FEIGENBAUM EVERY VISIT.

5. SHE WENT SOMEPLACE ON EAST 68TH STREET, AND TOOK A WAITING-ROOM MAGAZINE WITH HER.

6. SHE PLANS TO MOVE TO HER MOTHER'S IN DECEMBER.

7. SHE SAYS SHE IS INNOCENT.

8. HER THOUGHTS AND ATTENTION ARE ON SOMETHING ELSE.

9. SHE IS ON A DIET.

10. SHE REFUSES TO WEAR THE SILK DRESS MY MOTHER GAVE HER LAST CHRISTMAS.

11. SHE TAKES A LOT OF NAPS.

Harriet looked at the list, trying to decide what else to add, or whether she could rearrange the elements so they fell into a different order. Suddenly she saw an answer emerging. It was astounding, but if she added a few details that now seemed important, reworded some of the items, then deleted number 7, which still made no sense to her—

1. OLE GOLLY LEFT GEORGE WALDENSTEIN AND CAME TO NEW YORK IN MID-AUGUST.

2. SHE IS SAD AND DEPRESSED AND GROUCHY AND UNWELL.

3. SHE STARTED GOING REGULARLY TO SEE DR. FEIGENBAUM IN SEPTEMBER.*

4. SHE TAKES SOMETHING IN A BAG TO DR. FEIGENBAUM EVERY VISIT. (???)

5. SHE WENT ON A DIET, ALSO IN SEPTEMBER, AND STARTED TAKING NAPS.

6. SHE REFUSED TO WEAR THE BLUE SILK DRESS UNTIL THE SPRING.

7. SHE WENT SOMEPLACE WITH A WAITING ROOM IN EARLY NOVEMBER. (???)

8. SHE PLANS TO MOVE TO HER MOTHER'S IN DECEMBER.

9. HER THOUGHTS AND ATTENTION ARE ON SOMETHING ELSE. SOMETHING THAT HASN'T HAPPENED YET.

Harriet read the new list. Numbers 4 and 7 remained mysteries, so she deleted them in her mind. When she read the other items on the list, ignoring number 4 and number 7, everything fell into place and Harriet saw to her amazement exactly what was happening. It was so incredibly clear—but at the same time so incredibly unbelievable. Harriet was amazed that she hadn't figured it out before.

She decided to check out one very simple thing, the thing she had asterisked. Still in her pajamas, she put on her hiking boots and a heavy jacket and found her flashlight. Then she tiptoed down the stairs and quietly let herself out the front door.

Across the dark street Harriet stealthily climbed the front steps of the Feigenbaums' brownstone and stood next to the wrought-iron railing from which she had once toppled into the flowerbed. She clicked on the low beam of her flashlight and aimed it so it illuminated the bronze plaque to the left of the door, the plaque that said MORRIS FEIGENBAUM, M.D., and below it in smaller letters, PSYCHIATRY.

Harriet stood there in the same place where she had seen Ole Golly through her binoculars, where she had seen Ole Golly ring the Feigenbaums' doorbell and speak into the intercom.

Then she aimed her light a little higher, at the other bronze plaque, the one that had always been there, the one that quite clearly spelled out, in English, the information Harriet had ignored for much too long (The clue in the most obvious place! A Sherlock Holmes story had used the same device!): BARBARA FEIGENBAUM, M.D. Harriet hadn't been particularly interested in this doctor who dealt with women's medical problems. Psychiatry seemed more interesting. But now, below, in smaller letters, she read: OBSTETRICS AND GYNECOLOGY.

Ole Golly, Harriet realized, was going to have a baby.

CHAPTER 12

Harriet tried to think what to do now that she had figured out Ole Golly's secret.

Once, when Harriet was much younger and briefly attracted to dolls, a state of mind that had lasted about five minutes, her mother had bought her a tiny doll carriage and a doll cradle and a lot of fluffy doll clothes. The collection, Harriet remembered, had included teensy undershirts. She had played with everything one rainy afternoon in her room. While she was trying in frustration to force the stiff arm of a doll into one of the little knit undershirts, Harriet had glanced over toward her bedroom bookcase and noticed a copy of *Little House on the Prairie*, which she had received for her seventh birthday but had not yet read.

She remembered that she had thought suddenly, What would I rather be doing? Putting a dumb undershirt on a doll and then putting the doll into a little bed and pretending it goes to sleep so that then it will wake up and I can put a different undershirt on it? Or reading a book?

Harriet had given up dolls that very instant.

Babies, she knew, were not like dolls. They had bendable arms and loud cries and wet, gurgly smiles, and you could not leave them in a corner of the bedroom in a heap while you went to the movies. You could not leave them in a corner in a heap for one single minute, ever. They needed stuff. They needed food, and—

What was it, Harriet thought suddenly, that Ole Golly had said not terribly long ago? Something about what every child needs? It had made her seem very sad at the time.

Adequate health care was one thing. Well, Ole Golly's baby would probably have that, even if it had to live in Far Rockaway. They had vitamins in Far Rockaway.

Access to education. It would have that, too. Ole Golly had gone to public school and learned good penmanship and lots of poetry. Her baby could do the same.

What was the third thing? The thing that had made Ole Golly turn away and rush to her room?

Strictness. Well, her baby would *certainly* have that. Ole Golly would be nagging it about manners and posture all the time.

But it wasn't just strict that she had said, Harriet recalled. It was *strict and loving*. Not a problem. Ole Golly loved everything except Chinese food and violent movies.

Then Harriet remembered. *Parents*. Strict but loving *parents* was what Ole Golly had said. That was why she had rushed away and closed her door and maybe even cried.

That was the source of Ole Golly's sadness. Her baby wouldn't have parents.

Unless Harriet M-for-middle Welsch stepped in.

She decided to think of a way to make things right.

* * *

"Bonjour, ma petite!"

"Hello, Mother," Harriet said into the phone. Automatically she looked at her watch.

"What time—"

"It's one in the afternoon." Harriet had given up trying to make her mother remember the time difference.

"And the day is? I'm testing your *français*, darling."

"Dimanche." Sunday. Harriet had learned the days of the week in fifth grade.

"And the date?"

"Ah, let me think. *Novembre. Le septe.*" The seventh. "How are you, Mother? And Daddy?"

*"Nous sommes très, très—*Oh damn, Harriet, I can't think of it in French. We're just fine."

Harriet twiddled her marking pen. She was sitting cross-legged in the hall at the top of the stairs. Her time line was once again extended across the floor, weighted at each end to hold it flat, and she was sitting with her behind on AGE SIX. She had been adding a notation called APPEARANCE under each age, with a one-word description, and was thinking about gluing on a photograph as well, though she was afraid glued snapshots might make it difficult to roll up the time line.

"Can you think of a one-word description of me at age eight, Mother?"

"Age eight? Let me think. That would have been

four years ago. You were intelligent, industrious, organized—"

"*Appearance*, Mother."

"Oh, well, let me think. That was the year you grew so much but didn't gain any weight. So you were very thin for a while. I guess I would say *string bean*."

Harriet's pen had been poised under AGE EIGHT: APPEARANCE, but she could not bring herself to write a vegetable there.

"*String bean* is two words. Could you think of just one?"

"Tall," Harriet's mother said.

"Could you maybe think of a more interesting adjective than just *tall*?"

"Thin."

Harriet sighed and put her pen down.

"Darling, I'm glad I've been helpful with your project, but that's not really why I called. Guess what?"

"What?" Harriet was trying to think of a better word than *tall*, but nothing was coming to mind except *elongated*, and that just didn't seem right.

"We've made our reservations to come home! Your father's work here is just about finished. We'll fly back to New York on the twenty-second. The *vingt*—oh dear, the *vingt*—"

"*Vingt-deux*," Harriet supplied. In her mind she was thinking: *beanstalk?* But that was not an adjective. *Beanstalkish?* She didn't like the sound or look of it.

"So we'll be there just before Thanksgiving! In time for a real celebration! Is Miss Golly around, Harriet?"

"She's in her room. I think she's taking a nap."

"A nap! It's seven P.M., Harriet! Why is she taking a nap?"

"Mother, it's six hours earlier here."

"Of course it is. Silly me. Knock on her door, darling. I want her to make some arrangements for a big Thanksgiving dinner. I'm going to have her invite the Connellys. Their boys will be home from school—"

Harriet groaned.

"Be sweet, darling, Sylvia Connelly is my dearest friend."

"Well, if we have to have the Connellys, could we invite Sport?"

"Simon? Of course. And his lovely father."

"His father's married now. So can we invite his

lovely stepmother, too? Her name is Kate. They could bring pies."

"Of course, darling!"

Harriet had been pondering and pondering Ole Golly's problem. "Mother," she said tentatively, "if I invite one other person as a sort of surprise guest, would that be all right?"

She heard silence on the telephone. Finally her mother said, "Darling, I don't think a homeless person would fit in very comfortably with the Connellys."

"Not one of the homeless, Mother. Not this time. It's a homed person. I humbly beg."

"Oh dear. Someone from school, I assume. I suppose so, Harriet, but do make certain it's someone with good manners."

"It is, Mother, I promise. This person has extremely good manners. Very old-fashioned."

"All right, then. Get Miss Golly now, would you, darling?"

Harriet reached over and tapped on Ole Golly's door. "Could you come and talk to my mother on the phone?" she called. She heard Ole Golly's footsteps, and after a moment the door opened. Ole Golly was wearing her tweed bathrobe and her hair was flattened on one side. She blinked. Harriet handed her the telephone.

"Before you start talking to my mother, could you give me a one-word description of me at age eight? An adjective?"

Ole Golly looked down at the time line. She wrinkled her forehead the way she always did when she was thinking hard. *"Lissome,"* she said after a moment. "You were quite lissome at eight."

It was exactly right. "Thank you, dearest Ole Golly!" Harriet said enthusiastically. She rose to her knees and spread her arms in a dramatic gesture.

Ole Golly, holding the telephone, backed away with a look of dismay. "No hugging," she said firmly.

* * *

Harriet chewed on her tomato sandwich and half-listened to her school friends talking in the lunchroom.

"What are you guys doing for Thanksgiving?" Beth Ellen asked. "We have to go out to our house in Water Mill. It's going to be so boring."

"We're going to my grandparents' in Scarsdale," Carrie Andrews said. "We do that every Thanksgiving. All my cousins are always there. And this year it won't be boring at all because my cousin Kathleen just dropped out of Vassar to be a singer with a band so everybody's all upset. There will be a lot of yelling."

"What band?" Beth Ellen asked.

"Yeah, what band?" Rachel asked. Everyone looked very interested. Harriet finished her last bite of sandwich and stared out the window, thinking about how boring talk about bands was.

Carrie shrugged. "It's called Pustule but nobody's ever heard of it. And they're not even paying Kathleen anything. My uncle Harold says he's cutting off her allowance."

"She'll end up a homeless person," Beth Ellen said. "That's really awful. She should stay at college."

Everyone nodded. Everyone except Harriet. Harriet's mother had graduated from Vassar and Harriet had never figured out why that was such a fine thing. She thought she would probably drop out, too, if they made her go there. Harriet had no interest in being a band singer—it would interfere with her plans to become a spy, and anyway, she couldn't carry a tune very well—but she definitely thought people should pursue their dreams.

She said it aloud. "People should pursue their dreams."

"Even if they take your allowance away?" Carrie asked in amazement.

"Even if," Harriet said. "I know *I'm* going to pursue my dreams." She began to crumple her napkin and lunch bag.

" '*Dreams,*' " a voice said behind her, " '*which are the children of an idle brain, begot of nothing but vain fantasy*—' "

Harriet sighed. Only one person besides Ole Golly was in the habit of quoting all the time. She recognized the voice of her homeroom teacher, who also taught English and coached the drama club. "Is that Shakespeare?" she asked suspiciously, turning around. "It sounds like Shakespeare."

"*Romeo and Juliet,* act one, scene four," Mr. Grenville replied with a cheerful grin. He was wearing a teal-blue cashmere sweater today, and a bow tie with yellow polka dots.

"I don't have an idle brain," Harriet told him.

"You certainly don't, Harriet," he said. "You have a working-overtime brain and a very good heart as well. That's why I was looking for you. I need your help with something."

Harriet tossed her crumpled papers toward the trash can and missed. From behind the lunch counter, Mrs. McNair, who served hot lunch, glared at her. Mrs. McNair *always* glared at Harriet because she thought a steady diet of tomato sandwiches was unhealthy. "Greens," she always muttered when Harriet walked past. "You need greens."

"Yammer yammer yammer," Harriet always murmured in reply.

She picked up her trash from the floor and deposited it in the container. "What do you need help with?" she asked Mr. Grenville as she followed him from the lunchroom. "I mean, '*In what way might I be of assistance to your admirable self?*' That's Shakespeare."

"Baloney," Mr. Grenville said with a grin. "What play?"

Harriet thought quickly. "Ah, *Much Ado about Midsummer,*" she said. "Act seven."

He laughed. "Good fake, Harriet! You really do have a working-overtime brain. And by the time you finish at this school I will have drummed some Shakespeare into it so that you won't have to fake it."

"I'm getting better at faking, though, aren't I?" She followed Mr. Grenville into his empty classroom.

"Yes, you're quite good. You have a devious mind. You'll be an excellent secret agent." Harriet had written her sixth-grade Career Day report on the world of espionage.

Career Day had been a disappointment to Harriet. Adults—many of them parents of students, or aunts or uncles—had come to describe their careers to Gregory School students. There had been two doctors, one of whom had to leave in the middle of a panel discussion because she was called away by an emergency; an architect, who showed drawings and talked much too much about elevations; a retired baseball manager; an aging Broadway star who wore too much makeup (she was someone's grandmother); a man who owned a seafood restaurant; two professors of political science; one chemist; and seventeen lawyers. There were also three writers, and Harriet attended their panel discussion because she did plan to include writing as a part of her career. But the writers (one was Sport's father) were all shy, and they mumbled. And there had not been a single spy. Not one.

Mr. Grenville was looking through his briefcase, which he stored under his desk. "Here," he said, pulling out some papers. He placed the papers in a folder. "I was cleaning out my filing cabinet and I came across these papers that I should have returned to Simon Rocque at the end of school last June. I know he's a friend of yours, Harriet. I wonder if you could give these to him."

Harriet took the folder. "Sure," she said. "I see him all the time. He's coming to my house for Thanksgiving, actually, with his father and step-mother. They're bringing the pies."

"Really?" Mr. Grenville looked surprised. "I thought your parents were in France, Harriet. I was wondering if maybe you'd fly over to Paris for Thanksgiving. I was jealous, actually."

"Nope. They're coming back on Wednesday the twenty-second, the day before Thanksgiving. So we're having a big Thanksgiving dinner at our house, and the Rocques are coming, and also"— Harriet sighed—"the Connellys."

"You don't sound enthusiastic about the Connellys."

"They have rude sons," Harriet explained, "named for Shakespeare characters."

Mr. Grenville looked interested. "Don't tell me. Let me guess. Ah, Duncan and Horatio?"

"No, Malcolm and Edmund. They're both really finks. But Sylvia Connelly is my mother's best friend, so sometimes we have to put up with her children." She tucked the folder into her backpack. "And I hope one other person is coming, but I haven't invited him yet."

Mr. Grenville glanced at his watch. "Almost time for class," he said. "So I won't keep you. But I wanted to ask you one other favor, Harriet." He opened his desk drawer and began to look through some papers.

"Sure."

"After the Thanksgiving break, we have a new student entering school. She'll be in my homeroom, along with you and all your friends. It's very unusual to enter the Gregory School midyear. But apparently there are some difficult circumstances. Anyway, I was hoping you'd be willing to take her under your wing, Harriet."

Under my wing? Harriet thought. She pictured the page in her notebook she had titled DUMB PHRASES.

She decided that at the first possible opportunity she would add UNDER YOUR WING to the list. But she said, "Of course," politely to Mr. Grenville.

"Here," he said, finding the official paper he'd

been looking for in his desk drawer. "Her name is—let's see—Annie. Annie Smith. And, what else, she's twelve years old, her health is good, and blah blah blah. Here: under *interests* it says she likes to read. That's what made me think of you. If her interest had been science, I would have asked Janie to look out for her, or if her interest had been fashion, I would have asked—"

"Rachel, Carrie, Marion, Laura—"

"Right." He laughed. "Okay, thanks, Harriet. I knew I could count on you."

That one would go on her list, too, Harriet thought. COUNT ON YOU. Right below UNDER YOUR WING.

She turned to go.

"Carry on," Mr. Grenville said cheerfully.

That one, too: CARRY ON. Harriet searched her list for the appropriate reply.

"You betcha," she said.

*   *   *

"Hi, H'spy!"

"Oh, hello! I wasn't expecting you to call," Harriet said. "I thought I always had to call you, and give that one-ring signal."

"Well, I was bored, and hoping you would call, but you didn't."

"I started to," Harriet explained, "but the weather's so awful that I knew I couldn't come meet you in the alley."

"Look through your bedroom window, toward my house," Rosarita said.

"Wait." Harriet stretched the telephone cord and went to her window. Outside it was raining and cold. But through the rain, across the street, she could see Rosarita Sauvage in a third-floor window. Harriet waved.

"Is that your bedroom?" Harriet asked.

"My cell."

Harriet gulped. She wondered if perhaps psychiatrists sometimes had locked wards in their homes for mentally ill patients.

"But you go to school. And you can go out in the yard, and you've met me in the alley. Do they just lock you up at night? And how come they let you have a telephone?"

"Don't pry, H'spy."

"Well," Harriet added, after a pause, "thank you for calling. I hope you have a nice Thanksgiving."

"Wait, don't hang up!"

Harriet realized suddenly that she had the same feeling about Rosarita Sauvage that she did about Ole Golly. Beneath their grouchy and abrupt exteriors, Harriet understood, they were lonely. And frightened.

CHAPTER 13

"I can't believe it's snowing," Harriet said to Cook and Ole Golly at breakfast. From the kitchen window, high up on the wall, she could watch people's booted feet make their way with difficulty through deep slush. The last two days of school before Thanksgiving vacation had been canceled when the cold rain had turned to relentless snow.

"The weather patterns are changing everywhere," Ole Golly commented, looking up from the newspaper. "Tens of millions of people may be forced from low-lying areas as the seas rise. I read it in the paper last week."

"The seas rise? You read that?" said Cook. She set down a bowl of fresh cranberries. She'd been picking through them, discarding the wrinkled ones, preparing to cook them with orange slices and cinnamon to create her special cranberry sauce. It was still two days until Thanksgiving, but Cook always began her preparations early.

"Humanity is responsible," Ole Golly said. "The article blames humanity." She turned a page of the paper and sipped her tea.

"You and I are part of humanity," Harriet pointed out, "and we didn't do anything wrong. I don't know why they blame us. We recycle."

"Maybe it's all that paper you're wasting with those notebooks of yours," accused Cook. "How many notebooks have you gone through now? Must be hundreds. You're killing trees left and right." Cook emphasized this by throwing first her left arm and then her right out to her sides, endangering the spice rack and making Harriet quite indignant.

"Well, you're the one polluting the air with all your cigarette smoke," Harriet shot back. "And there's enough onion in your meat loaf to choke a horse!"

"That's quite enough now," Ole Golly said. "We have a lot of things to do to prepare for Thanksgiving. Get to work."

"I'm going to set the table with Mother's best

tablecloth and silverware. Tell me again how many people." Harriet took her cereal bowl to the sink.

Cook picked up the bowl of cranberries and set to work again. "You and your mama and daddy," she said. "That's three."

"Sport and his father and Kate," Harriet added. "That makes six."

"The Connellys." Ole Golly said it with disdain.

"Yes, the Connellys, all four of them. That's ten," Harriet said. "And Mother gave me permission to invite another person, so that's eleven. And you and Cook make thirteen. I'm going to use those white plates with the gold edge."

"Count me out," Cook said. "With all these people coming, I'll be so busy in the kitchen, I'll be lucky to sit down at all."

"Make it eleven places, Harriet," Ole Golly said. "I'll keep Cook company in the kitchen."

"Why?" Harriet asked.

"I won't want to eat much. And I'm not feeling very sociable lately." She reached for the Lincoln Center coffee mug by the telephone and found a pencil. Then she folded *The New York Times* so the crossword puzzle was positioned just right. There was no talking to Ole Golly, Harriet knew, once she had started the puzzle.

* * *

"Why exactly aren't you feeling sociable lately, Ole Golly?" Harriet asked that afternoon. She had waited for a quiet moment. The crossword puzzle was completed. The table was set for eleven people, and Harriet had even made place cards and arranged them so Malcolm and Edmund Connelly would be as far away from her as possible.

Now they were sitting in the library after their snack. There was a fire in the fireplace, and outside snow still swirled and wind whistled in the street. Cook, bundled into boots and scarf and heavy down coat, had left early to make her way to Brooklyn by subway.

"What if you can't get back, Cooky? I don't know how to make stuffing. Maybe you should spend the night here tonight," Harriet had suggested as Cook zipped her plush-lined boots.

But Cook shook her head. "I got here this morning, and I'll get back tomorrow. The subway will be running. But I have to be home tonight to get Junior's dinner. He's had a bad attitude lately. I think he's been eating junk food."

Harriet thought about the children she might have if she decided to have children. Vladimir and

Francesca. What if they were pale and weak, like Pinky Whitehead? Or snobby and materialistic, like Rachel and Marion? What if, like Junior, they had a personality disorder? Or talked dirty, like the Connellys? What if they stole? Oh dear. According to Cook, a mother would love them anyway, no matter what, but it would certainly be hard. According to Cook, it wasn't always easy to be a mother. Maybe, Harriet decided, she would devote her life solely to spying.

She wondered what kind of mother Ole Golly would be. Sport had gotten along with no real mother just fine. But Ole Golly wanted her child to have parents. She decided not to think about this now.

Ole Golly was just finishing the final part of Harriet's sweater, the left sleeve. Harriet had held her arm out for measuring several times. Her left arm, she had discovered, was a quarter of an inch shorter than her right. This was an interesting anatomical fact. Harriet had always admired the symmetry of her feet, but now she was concerned that it might be an optical illusion and that her feet might not actually match. She intended to measure all the other parts of her body to see if the same discrepancy occurred, and if it did, she was going to write to the American Medical Association about it. So far she had only done her nostrils, and they seemed to be equal, though it was hard to tell with nostrils because they didn't exactly hold still. That was why there were so many interesting nostril verbs, like *quiver* and *flare*.

Ole Golly sighed when Harriet asked why she wasn't feeling sociable. "Because I'm tired," she said, and knit a few more stitches.

Harriet had hoped that Ole Golly was ready to confess, to say, "Because I'm pregnant, because I am bringing an innocent child into the world in a dumpy house in Far Rockaway where my mother says *ain't*," and then she and Harriet could discuss it. Harriet watched the cuff of the sweater turn slowly in Ole Golly's hands. She tried to maneuver the conversation.

"Are you tired of your job?" she asked after a moment.

"My job? I don't have a job," Ole Golly said, lifting her eyebrows. Harriet noticed that Ole Golly's eyebrows seemed to be exactly the same size. She wondered about her own and glanced toward the tape measure.

"Yes, you do. Taking care of me."

Ole Golly snipped a piece of yarn with her tiny scissors. "I have a *position* here. That is not the same thing. And no, I am not at all tired of it. I am grateful for it."

Harriet picked up the narrow yellow tape measure that Ole Golly used for her knitting. She held one end to her left eyebrow. "Well, are you tired of New York?" she asked.

"No. I'm tired of the photography gallery of the Museum of Modern Art; it's too confusing. I'm tired of taxi drivers: too impolite. Times Square: too many tourists. Bloomingdale's: too expensive. And certain movie theaters that poison the mind. But I avoid them. On the whole, I like New York very much," Ole Golly said.

Harriet held the measuring tape across her left eyebrow carefully. She stood and went to the mirror over the fireplace. The numbers were backward in the mirror, but she could read them if she set her mind to it. Her left eyebrow seemed to be 1.6 inches horizontally, but that didn't account for the slight arch. Harriet tried to make the tape measure curve slightly to match the brow.

"Were you tired of Montreal?" she asked. The tape measure uncurled and dangled in front of her eyes, making it difficult to read the number over her eyebrow.

Ole Golly said no. "I liked Montreal," she said. "It's pretty there." While Harriet watched in the mirror, Ole Golly turned the sweater inside out and looked at the many bits of dangling yarn. From her little zippered bag she took a needle and threaded one of the yarn bits into its large eye. Carefully she began to weave the yarn into the inside of the sweater, where it wouldn't show.

Harriet gave up on her eyebrows. She replaced the tape measure in Ole Golly's knitting basket. Trying to sound casual, she asked, "Were you tired of Mr. Waldenstein?"

From below on the street, they could hear the squealing whir of a tire caught on freezing snow. Harriet glanced down through the window and watched a yellow taxi rock back and forth as the driver tried to get it loose; finally it eased away and continued slowly down the snowy street. There was not another vehicle in sight.

"Harriet, I was not going to discuss this with you. But I will tell you that George Waldenstein misrepresented himself," Ole Golly said suddenly. "I was not at all tired of him. But a person does not tolerate deception."

"But how—"

"Enough. Nothing more will be forthcoming on that topic."

When Ole Golly spoke firmly, she was not to be budged, Harriet knew. She sat down and stared at the fire, which flickered blue and orange.

"Are you tired of *me?*" she asked at last.

"Only of your questions," Ole Golly said with a sigh. "Here." She tossed the finished sweater to Harriet. "Try this on."

* * *

"Pumpkin chiffon, with a crushed-gingersnap-and-pecan crust," Sport announced over the telephone. "And—"

"Wait," Harriet said. "I can't type very fast."

She began to add it to the list of food she was creating. She planned to type the menu for Thanksgiving dinner and place it in the center of the table the way a fine restaurant might.

Sport continued. "And I'm also making—"

"Wait," Harriet said again. She put the telephone receiver on the desk so she could use both hands. Then she typed:

PUMPKIN CHIFFON PIE

crushed-gingersnap-&-pecan crust

She looked at it and smiled. Then she typed an addition to it, so that it said:

PUMPKIN CHIFFON PIE

crushed-gingersnap-&-pecan crust à la Simon Rocque

"Sport," she told him, "you're going to be amazed. Okay, what else?"

"Apple pie."

Harriet typed some more.

APPLE PIE SIMONESQUE

"Just wait till you see this, Sport. This dinner is going to be so spectacular I don't even mind that the Connelly twins are coming."

"*I* mind," Sport grumbled. "They always torture me. They give me wedgies at every opportunity."

Harriet knew that. She had seen it happen. But she had decided that Thanksgiving would be wonderful despite the Connellys. "I'll tell my dad to keep an eye on them in case they try anything," she reassured Sport.

"Also," she said, "I have another idea. For the culmination of the celebration."

"The *pièce de résistance?*"

"You sound like my mother, Sport. But yes, that's exactly what it will be."

After Harriet hung up the phone, she worked some more on the menu.

COFFEE OR TEA

She had thought that would be the final notation, and maybe she could use a marking pen to make a decorative little swirl below it. But then she decided to add one more thing:

**VERY SPECIAL SURPRISE
IMMEDIATELY AFTER DINNER**

Harriet made certain Ole Golly was still in her bedroom with the door tightly closed. The house was silent. No one was eavesdropping. Through the window, she could see that across the street the Feigenbaums' house was dark, with the draperies drawn across the windows. The wind whistled in the snow-filled street below.

Harriet took a deep breath, picked up the phone, and dialed Montreal.

CHAPTER 14

Harriet recognized his voice when he answered the telephone. She had heard it often during those days last year when he had come shyly to the Welsches' house to woo Ole Golly. Despite the fact that his method of transportation was a delivery bike, George Waldenstein had been sweetly formal, carefully shaking out his creased trousers when he dismounted and saying "Good evening" to Harriet with a small nod, as if she were an adult.

She could almost picture his head making that bashful nod again as she identified herself. "Maybe you don't remember me—" she began.

"Good evening to you, Harriet," he said. "Of course I remember you. You were a wonderful companion to Catherine. And when I was privileged to be in your company, to me, as well. I recall that we once went to the cinema together."

Harriet smiled. "Yes, I remember that! We saw that movie where Paul Newman was Apollo, and I rode in the container on your delivery bike! It was more fun than anything!"

They were silent together for a moment, and Harriet knew somehow that they were both remembering one of the happiest nights of their lives. It had been the night that Mr. Waldenstein proposed to Ole Golly. Harriet hadn't known at the time. A proposal was a very private thing, as loving was. She had only known that riding there, curled in the delivery box with the lid down on top of her, and Ole Golly sitting primly behind George Waldenstein on the bike whisking them through New York on their way to the movies, they had all three been part of something very big and wonderful and filled with future.

Harriet thought for a moment that she might cry.

"It's snowing here," she said quickly. Talking about the weather was a good way to make tears go away.

"Here, too," George Waldenstein said, and she

heard him sniff and knew that he had been about to cry as well.

"*Il neige*," Harriet said, to show him that she knew a little French.

"*Oui, il neige.*"

Then they were silent.

"Mr. Waldenstein—"

"Harriet—"

They both laughed. "You first," George Waldenstein said politely.

Harriet plunged in. "Did you know that Ole Golly is here?" she asked. "I mean Catherine? I mean your wife?"

"Yes. She told me where she was going. If she hadn't, I would have been frantic with worry, Harriet. But I knew she was going to a good place."

"But you haven't called or anything! It's been three whole months since she came, and you haven't called once!"

"I promised her I wouldn't," he said solemnly.

"She's very, very sad," Harriet said. She had decided she could not tell Mr. Waldenstein about the baby. It was not her place. Only a wife could tell a husband that news. Sometimes in movies the wife knit a tiny sweater and showed it to the husband with a knowing smile, and then they hugged and violins played. Harriet hoped Ole Golly and George Waldenstein could have a scene like that. But first she had to get him to New York.

"So am I," George Waldenstein said, and Harriet could tell from his voice that it was true. "I, too, am very sad."

"Mr. Waldenstein, she told me just today—just this very afternoon—that she was not tired of you. That is the absolute truth. She said it."

She could hear him sigh. "That may be, Harriet, but she became tired of my deception. I misrepresented myself. There is no excuse. She was right to leave me."

"What did you do? What could have been that bad?" Harriet knew it was a nosy question, what Ole Golly would have called a busybody question. But she didn't care. She needed to know.

"I told her that we would go to Montreal to begin a wonderful life together. That we would buy a little convenience store, and we would perhaps live above it in a cozy flat. We pictured how she would be cooking dinner upstairs and I would be below, selling milk and potato chips and *la litière du chat* to people from the neighborhood—"

"I'm sorry but I don't know what that is. We haven't had that in vocabulary yet."

"Kitty litter," Mr. Waldenstein explained.

"Oh."

"—and small children would pop in to buy candy," he went on, "and we would know each one by name—that was important to Catherine, to be near children; she loves them so—"

His voice broke slightly.

"Oh, please don't cry, Mr. Waldenstein. Talk about the weather for a minute," Harriet suggested. Her own voice was a little shaky.

She heard him take a deep breath. "It seems to be changing to sleet here," he said.

"It's very windy here," Harriet said.

"The forecast is for much more snow," Mr. Waldenstein said.

"Yes, here, too. I think we already have six inches."

"All right, I can go on now," Mr. Waldenstein said in a stronger voice.

"Please do."

"So we pooled our savings and opened a bank account, and we moved in with my mother while we looked around for a shop with a flat above it."

"So far," Harriet commented, "I haven't heard anything about deception. Not a single word."

"My mother was very, very old," Mr. Waldenstein said. "She needed a lot of looking after."

"My goodness."

"And she was not very pleasant. I have to admit that, even though she was my mother. She was never pleasant, even when she was younger."

"That's very sad, Mr. Waldenstein. Did you deceive Ole Golly by pretending that your mother would be jolly and fun?"

He sighed. "No. I told Catherine that Mother would be difficult."

"So you didn't misrepresent anything."

"Well, nothing about Mother. Catherine said that she had certainly had to deal with unpleasant people before. She didn't mean you, Harriet—"

"No. But probably I was difficult occasionally when I was younger," Harriet acknowledged. "I had tantrums."

He sighed again. "So did Mother. Anyway, every day I set out to look at real estate and Catherine stayed with Mother, dressing her and feeding her, and being no-nonsense when Mother was particularly difficult. One day Mother threw a coffeepot at Catherine. It pains me to tell you this, Harriet."

"Was there hot coffee in it? Did she get scalded?" Harriet was horrified. She pictured poor Ole Golly burned and wet.

"No, it was empty. And Mother missed. Her aim wasn't good."

"Oh."

"Each evening I came home, and after Catherine got Mother put to bed, we would talk about our day. Sometimes we would have a small glass of wine. I would tell Catherine about the stores I had looked at, with flats above, but none of them was cozy enough for us, or the price was too high, or the neighborhood not good enough. Catherine was so patient. She was so certain that we would find just the right place. We would sit there sipping our wine, talking about how happy we would be in our own cozy place—"

"Oh dear." Harriet could hear his voice tremble again. "How's the weather now, Mr. Waldenstein? Still sleeting?"

"Yes. But they do predict sun by Saturday. That's only four days away."

"It's very windy here," Harriet said.

"I'm all right now."

"Go on, then. You were sipping wine, and talking about cozy flats—"

"Yes, each evening."

"Mr. Waldenstein, it doesn't sound as if you did anything wrong. It wasn't your fault about the coffeepot. Anyway, she missed."

"I'm getting to the hard part now, Harriet. Bear with me. The truth is, I never looked at a single convenience store, or any cozy flats, or even noncozy flats."

"Mr. Waldenstein! You were lying to Ole Golly!"

"Yes, dear heart, I was."

"But *why*?"

"Because I wanted it so badly: the store, the flat, the life we had imagined. But—oh dear; this is hard.

"The truth is, there was not enough money. Do you remember that I told you we pooled our savings and opened a bank account?"

"Yes."

"Well, it was all her savings. Dear Catherine's. I didn't have any savings at all. I had never earned enough as a deliveryman in New York. I had nothing. Nothing but my love for Catherine, and my hope that we—" He paused.

"It's very windy here, Mr. Waldenstein, and they say the snow will continue all through tomorrow."

She could hear him take several deep breaths. Then he continued. "So there was not enough money. Catherine had been very prudent, and your parents had paid her very well, but her savings were small. And I had none at all, though she didn't know that, because I had deceived her. So each day I went out, leaving her to tend that miserable mother of mine, dodging the things that were thrown at her. Once it was a box of raisin bran, I remember."

"But what did you *do* each day, Mr. Waldenstein, if you weren't looking for a convenience store with a cozy flat above?"

"I tried to *get* the money."

Harriet was shocked. "*Mr. Waldenstein!* You weren't robbing banks, were you?"

"No, of course not. Harriet, do you speak French?"

Harriet hesitated. "Well, you and I said '*Il neige*' to each other. And Cook thinks I do. I told Cook that I'm fluent in French. But I'm really not. I know some words, though."

"*La Poule aux Oeufs d'Or,*" Mr. Waldenstein said.

Harriet repeated it to herself but she didn't understand what it meant. "I give up," she said.

"The Hen that Lays Golden Eggs," he told her. "That's what I did every day."

"I don't get it. You took up chicken farming?"

"No, it's the name of one of the Canadian lottery

games. There are others. *Québec Banco*. Mini. *La Quotidienne*. I played them all."

"You *gambled?* And you were using Ole Golly's savings? Mr. Waldenstein!"

"Using Catherine's savings, and *losing* Catherine's savings. It's true," he said. "It was despicable. I just wanted it all so much." He fell silent.

"One time," Harriet told him, "I asked Ole Golly how it felt to be in love, and you know what she said?"

"Tell me," he said in a small voice.

"She said it felt as if doors were opening all over the world. She said it was bigger than the world itself."

She could hear him begin to cry, and it was too sad a crying to be deflected by talk about the weather. Also, Harriet felt somehow that he *needed* the crying. Sometimes people did. Sometimes *she* did.

"I closed all those doors," he said when he could talk again.

"Yes, you did. You slammed them in her face. It wasn't fair."

"I ruined her life, and my own," George Waldenstein said.

"And now for punishment, you have to live with

your terrible mother and dodge when she throws things at you."

"No," he said, "my mother died two months ago. My punishment is living without Catherine. And to make it *worse*, my mother left me a good bit of money, so now I have the convenience store and the cozy flat. But it isn't cozy all alone. Every day I think about how it might have been." He gave a long sigh. Harriet sighed with him.

"Mr. Waldenstein?"

"Yes, dear heart?"

"Here's what I think you should do. Here's what you *must* do. You must take a plane to New York, and you must appear on our doorstep and ring the bell at exactly five P.M. on Thursday. I've written you onto the menu."

She could hear Mr. Waldenstein give a small sad laugh, not a happy one. Maybe, Harriet thought, recalling her list of adjectives, it was *rueful*.

"She would slam the door, Harriet, in a mad, thunking way. You know how she gets sometimes."

"But she *misses* you, Mr. Waldenstein! Take the chance! Sometimes you just have to take the chance and let the chips fall where they may." Even as she said it, Harriet knew that she would add LET THE CHIPS FALL WHERE THEY MAY to her list of dumb phrases.

"It's tempting, Harriet. But impossible. It's Thanksgiving in the U.S.A., you know."

"Of course I know. I've set a place for you—for dessert, not the main course. You're to be the *pièce de résistance*."

"Thank you, *ma chérie*. But I've been watching the news on television. And just today they were talking about how this is the busiest holiday in U.S. airports all year. There are no tickets available. All flights are overbooked. So although it is tempting— although for a moment you made me feel that it would be the right thing to do—it is impossible."

Harriet's heart sank, even though SINKING HEART was also on her list of dumb phrases. There was no hope. Her parents were arriving home, and Ole Golly was planning to move to Far Rockaway on the first of December, immediately after Thanksgiving. Spying, Harriet had seen that Ole Golly had taken her big suitcase out of the closet where it had been stored. Somehow she knew things could never be repaired once Ole Golly had moved to Far Rockaway.

"But she has something very important to tell you. And she's innocent, too," Harriet added glumly, not even knowing what Ole Golly was innocent *of*.

"*Pardon?*"

"I heard her say it, Mr. Waldenstein. She whispered it into the telephone to my mother, just like this: '*I'm innocent.*' No, wait. It was more like this: '*I'm innossssennnt.*' She sounded so scared."

Harriet could hear Mr. Waldenstein take a startled breath. For a moment he was silent. Then he said gruffly, "Harriet, I'll be there Thursday. I'll find a way. There must be a train."

CHAPTER 15

The silverware and plates were on the table, and the menu was propped in the center. Cook was in the kitchen, and outdoors it was still snowing. The drifts were mountainous, the streets were unplowed, and the snow was still falling.

And Harriet's parents, who had been due to arrive in New York earlier that day, were still not home.

"Darling," Mrs. Welsch had said to Harriet over the telephone, "*Quel dommage!* What an absolute shame! Here we are at Charles de Gaulle Airport, and they say there's a blizzard in New York, so our plane can't leave!"

"Cook's making the stuffing right now," Harriet said. "She put chestnuts in it."

"Well, it says DELAYED on the monitor, so we'll just sit here and wait. I'm certain we'll get there before long. Your father's in a foul mood, though, I must say."

Much later in the day, another call came from Paris.

"Is it really snowing there, or is all this just some big hoax because Air France doesn't feel like flying this plane?" Harriet's father demanded when she answered.

"It's really snowing hard, Dad."

"We've been sitting in this damn airport for six hours," he said. "Your mother is furious."

"I think the snow will stop before long, Dad." Harriet lied to reassure him. "The flakes are getting bigger." It was not true. Cook had reluctantly decided to spend the night because she was not at all certain she could even make it to Brooklyn.

"I'll tell her that, and maybe we'll tell Air France as well. The seats in this airport are incredibly uncomfortable."

Later, as Harriet was getting ready for bed, the telephone rang again. This time it was her mother.

"It's two in the morning here!" Mrs. Welsch said angrily. "Do you realize that? It probably feels like early evening to you, Harriet, but you're forgetting that there is a six-hour time difference! Do you understand that your parents are sitting in an airport at two A.M.? And they still won't tell us exactly when this plane is going to depart?"

"I'm sorry, Mother. I *do* know about the time difference."

"Your father is livid. I've never seen him so outraged. He's in the bar, drinking red wine. Oops. I must go, Harriet. They're making an announcement."

●　●　●

There was so much to do the next day that Harriet forgot to worry about her parents' plight. She brought the fancy serving dishes from the dining room cupboard to the kitchen and lined them up on the pine table so they would be ready for Cook to fill them with mashed potatoes and creamed onions and peas and gravy and all the things Harriet loved.

Yeasty dough for rolls had been rising in a blue bowl covered with a cloth, and now Harriet watched as Cook poked at it one more time, shaped the dough into crescents, placed them in neat rows on a baking sheet, and covered them again.

"I'll never bother learning to cook, because I won't need to. I'll always be off on spying assignments, probably in Eastern Europe or the Mideast," Harriet commented.

"Even spies eat."

"Yes, but they never cook. They eat in restaurants."

"News to me. I never knew a spy. Except you, of course, Harriet. Hey, *watch it*. Don't go sticking your fingers into everything." Cook slapped at Harriet's hand.

"It was just the smidgeniest smidgen of cranberry sauce," Harriet said. She sucked on her finger.

"What time is it?" Cook asked.

"Three o'clock. Why don't you ever look at the clock like a normal person?"

"If I was a normal person, Harriet Welsch, I would be in Brooklyn with my family on Thanksgiving. Put some olives in a bowl. Use that nice crystal one there. People are going to be arriving soon."

"*We gather together to ask the Lord's blessing,*" Harriet sang loudly as she filled the small crystal bowl with olives from a jar.

"*He hastens and chastens his will to make known,*" Cook joined in with her big trembling voice.

The doorbell rang. "Ole Golly?" Harriet called up the stairs. "Can you answer the door?"

But there was no reply. Ole Golly had gone to her room after breakfast and had not emerged. "I have packing to do," she had announced. "I'll be busy in my room."

"Ole Golly is depressed," Harriet had said to Cook after Ole Golly left the kitchen.

"Holidays always bring on depression," Cook had said, "or make it worse. Junior is feeling very depressed."

The doorbell rang again. At the same moment the telephone rang. Cook and Harriet looked at each other. "I'll do the door," Cook decided. She wiped her hands on her apron. Harriet picked up the phone.

"Darling?" Her mother's voice was staticky.

"Mother? Where are you? Are you still in Paris?" Upstairs Harriet could hear Simon and his parents entering and stamping snow from their boots.

"No, we've made it to Hartford. The storm doesn't seem to have hit quite as hard here yet. Oh! They're announcing the final call for our flight to New York. Daddy is very anxious for us to board the plane. But I just wanted to let you know we're on our way."

Harriet heard the Rocques go into the living room. "People are arriving, Mother!"

"Yes, we'll be arriving in just a few hours, dear," Mrs. Welsch said in a sprightly voice. "They say the planes are all stacked up because flights from all over were delayed."

"What about trains, Mother? Do you know if trains are delayed, too?"

"Harriet, you silly thing. We couldn't have taken a train from Paris!"

"I just heard the Rocques arrive, Mother. I have to go," Harriet said.

"Of course you do, darling! Don't wait dinner for us, but we'll be there before too terribly long. We have a limo waiting at the airport. Oh, wait, Harriet, Daddy is saying something to me."

Harriet waited. Because Cook was out of the room, she reached over and poked her finger into the cranberry sauce. She licked it quickly. She could hear Cook coming down the stairs.

"What did Daddy want? I have to hang up."

"He wanted to tell me to hang up, darling; we're about to miss our flight. See you soon!"

Harriet hung up and licked her finger one more time as Cook entered the kitchen carrying the two pies Sport had made.

"The Rocques came on skis, Harriet. Damnedest thing I ever saw! On skis and carrying pies!

"I served the grown-ups some wine. Go be sociable, and see if you can get Miss Golly to come down. We'll be eating in another half hour. I hope the Connellys can get here. I wonder if they ski. There aren't any taxis."

"*We gather together . . .*" Harriet began the Thanksgiving song again. She marched up the stairs, singing, and greeted Sport and his parents, who were rosy-cheeked and hungry.

"It wasn't easy, Harriet," Sport said, "carrying those pies on skis. I think the crust got cracked on one."

Harriet continued to the second floor and then the third, still singing. "*He forgets not his own,*" she concluded loudly, and knocked on Ole Golly's door.

"Time to come down and see everybody!" Harriet called cheerfully. "And then dinner, and then who knows what might happen *after* dinner? There might be a surprise! A *pièce de résistance!*"

Ole Golly opened the door. Behind her, on the bed, Harriet could see the open suitcase. She could see folded underwear in it. She averted her eyes quickly. It felt rude to look at Ole Golly's underwear.

"My parents are in Hartford!" Harriet added.

Ole Golly sighed.

"Look! I'm wearing the sweater you made me!" Harriet posed, modeling the colorful sweater. "Are you knitting anything new? Maybe something, ah, small? Why don't you bring your knitting downstairs with you?" She peered at Ole Golly's knitting basket on the floor beside the chair, trying to see if some tiny garment was in progress. If so, Ole Golly could shyly hold up a small pink or pale blue sweater as a way of announcing things to Mr. Waldenstein, just the way—was it Doris Day?—had in an old movie once.

"*Over the river and through the woods*," she sang as she descended the stairs. Harriet M. Welsch knew a lot of Thanksgiving songs.

The Connellys called at 4:37 and said they would not make it.

Harriet graciously accepted their regrets over the phone. Then, after hanging up, she did a little dance. "Thank you, snooow!" she sang.

Ole Golly came downstairs, wearing her things, and sat in the living room with Sport's parents. She sipped a few sips of wine. Harriet pulled Sport aside and whispered to him in the hall.

"George Waldenstein promised he'd be here at five. He's the *pièce de résistance*. But look out the window, Sport! There's not a single cab on the streets. He'll never make it!"

"It's already five, Harriet. Weren't we supposed to eat at four? I'm hungry!"

Cook called in a low voice from the stairs to the kitchen. "This turkey's practically ruined, Harriet! I think we ought to serve dinner!"

So Harriet and the Rocques arranged themselves at the table set for eleven. Ole Golly joined them after all, so only one of the places set for Harriet's parents was empty. The four places set for the Connellys were empty. The place set for the mystery guest was empty.

Cook served the turkey and someone began to pass the bowl of mashed potatoes. Outside, it had begun to get dark, in the eerie way that darkness comes through snow. Streetlights came on and made cones of golden light, through which the snow continued to swirl.

At 5:22, as Harriet spooned gravy onto her plate, she heard the doorbell ring. She heard Cook head across the kitchen and up the stairs to the front door.

She glanced at Ole Golly, who was buttering a roll and talking to Kate Rocque about a poetry reading that Kate had attended at the Ninety-second

Street Y. She glanced at Sport and grinned. Sport grinned back. It *had* to be George Waldenstein at the door. Her parents had keys and wouldn't ring the bell. The Connellys had said they weren't coming. There was no one else.

"*Harriet!*" Cook's voice was urgent, and it wasn't just a Harriet-get-your-butt-down-here-now voice. Cook was scared. "*Miss Golly!* I need help! Hurry!"

They heard a large thump on the hall floor above.

*   *   *

Harriet was very glad that Morris Feigenbaum answered the door. She had been worried that she might have to deal with Rosarita Sauvage and a lot of frivolous, mysterious conversation directed at H'spy. But the psychiatrist himself was the one who came at last in answer to her desperate repeated punching of the buzzer.

"We're in the middle of our Thanksgiving dinner," he said, looking down at Harriet not unkindly.

"I know!" Harriet told him. "Everyone is! But we need a doctor! We need you right away, across the street! And your wife!"

Dr. Feigenbaum's face had a puzzled what-on-earth-are-you-talking-about look.

"It's an emergency!" Harriet explained. "George Waldenstein came all the way from Montreal by train, and he got to Penn Station and there were no taxis, so he took the subway to Fifty-ninth Street, and he waited and waited but the number four train didn't come, or the five, or the six—none of them came, I suppose because it's Thanksgiving and it's a blizzard—and he had promised, absolutely promised, that he'd be here by five P.M. because he's to be the *pièce de résistance*, so he started walking, and the snow is a foot deep, but Mr. Waldenstein is only five feet tall, and he kept falling over, so he kept saying to himself, 'Catherine, Catherine,' just like the guy in that movie, *Wuthering Heights?* And he got up again, and up again, and finally he made it to our front door, but he's covered in snow and he can't unbend, and his lips are blue, and—oh please, just come!"

"Well," Dr. Feigenbaum said, after thinking it over, "let me put on some boots."

"Dr. Feigenbaum," Harriet implored, "you can walk where my feet were. See? I made deep holes in the snow. You don't have time to put on boots!"

He looked at Harriet, looked at her foot holes in the snow, and sighed. "Holidays are tough. People always seem to have these problems in the middle of holiday dinners," he said, grumbling slightly. He reached for a small medical bag that was on the hall floor. "But all right. Lead on.

"Barbara!" he called up the stairs. "Medical emergency across the street, at the Welsches'!"

He followed Harriet through the snow back to the Welsches' house. Cook was standing in the front hall wringing her hands in her apron.

"Your parents called from Connecticut," Cook told Harriet. "The storm did hit Hartford, so their plane couldn't take off. They're stuck and they're in a very bad mood. I didn't even tell them about *this*."

This was George Waldenstein, horizontal on the hall floor. Ole Golly was on her knees beside him on the Oriental rug, gently rubbing his face. He was looking up at her with affection, embarrassment, and chattering teeth. The rest of him was still encased in snow.

Dr. Morris Feigenbaum was reaching into his bag of medical equipment just as the door opened again and Dr. Barbara Feigenbaum appeared. "What's going on?" she said. "Morris, why did *you* come? Catherine's *my* patient!" Then she saw Ole Golly kneeling on the floor. "Catherine? What is it? Are you all right? You're not due until April! And who's this?"

"It's my husband!" Ole Golly said. "He came all the way from Montreal to bring me this. It was his when he was a baby." She pried open the stiffened fingers of Mr. Waldenstein's right hand, removed the snow-covered object he was holding, and held it up. It was a little silver cup with the name GEORGIE engraved on the side.

"That reminds me. I got your amnio results," Barbara Feigenbaum said as she leaned down to examine Mr. Waldenstein. "I wrote myself a note to call you on Monday. Georgie won't do. It's a girl."

"A girl!" Ole Golly said. She leaned over Mr. Waldenstein's frozen face. "George? Did you hear? We're having a baby, and—"

He fluttered his eyelids. There were little icicles in his eyelashes. "I know," he said, shivering. "Harriet told me."

"I didn't! I swear I didn't! I wanted Ole Golly to be the one to tell you! I wanted her to hold up a little knitted garment!" Harriet insisted. "The only thing I told you, Mr. Waldenstein, was that Ole Golly missed you and that she was innocent!"

"Harriet, I didn't say *innocent*. I said *enceinte*, which is French for *pregnant*. I was afraid you might be listening in on my phone conversation with your mother."

Then Ole Golly turned to her husband. "It's true, George," she said. "I'm *enceinte*." She stroked his face affectionately, and Harriet could see that it wasn't quite as blue as it had been. "Try to wiggle your upper lip, dear," Ole Golly instructed him. "See if you can break your mustache."

Simon Rocque was plugging a hair dryer into an electrical outlet at the foot of the stairs. "Stand back, everyone," he said. "I'm going to melt him."

· · ·

The house was quiet. Carefully Sport cut the pies and Harriet passed the slices around. The Rocques were back at the table, and now the two Dr. Feigenbaums were there, as well, waiting attentively to make certain that Mr. Waldenstein didn't relapse into frozenness. Cook had joined them at the table, too. Upstairs, George Waldenstein, melted, wearing Harriet's father's pajamas, was tucked into Harriet's parents' bed, under Harriet's parents' electric blanket. Ole Golly was holding his hand and giving him small sips of tea with brandy in it.

"This is yummy, Sport," Kate said. "Truly yummy."

Sport beamed. "More, anyone?" he offered.

The doorbell rang abruptly. Then they could hear the unlocked door pushed open, and footsteps in the hall. "Where *is* everybody?" a vaguely familiar voice called, and the footsteps stomped toward the dining room.

"I got left sitting all alone in front of a turkey!" the girl said angrily from the doorway. "Like I'm supposed to know how to carve? What's going on?"

Sport, standing in front of a half-eaten pumpkin chiffon pie, gasped and stammered, "Yo—Yolanda Montezuma!"

Harriet faced the girl and demanded, "What are you doing in my house, Rosarita Sauvage? You said you were being held prisoner!"

The girl frowned. "My name at the moment is Zoe Carpaccio, and I'm looking for my family. They all dashed out into the snow and left me sitting there like a stupe. Now I find them lounging around eating pie. What kind of pie is that? It looks good. I'll have a piece. Pass the pie, H'spy.

"And by the way," she said to Harriet, "how do you do? I'm actually Annie Smith. I'm starting at your school on Monday. The guy there said maybe you'd walk with me, so I've already put it on my time line: STARTING SCHOOL WITH HARRIET M. WELSCH."

"Your time line?" Harriet said. "I thought I was the only person with a time line!"

* * *

"So," Harriet said, pointing, "I listed the most important things for each year. Firsts. See this? LOSES FIRST TOOTH? Under AGE SIX?"

She was kneeling on her bedroom floor with Annie while they examined her time line.

"I put you here, under AGE ELEVEN, but now I have to figure out how to change it. Maybe I can use Wite-Out." Harriet rubbed her finger along the phrase MEETS ROSARITA SAUVAGE.

"Don't change it," Annie said. "You *did* meet me when I was being Rosarita. I still am Rosarita sometimes, when I'm feeling savage."

"Did you know that *sauvage* means *fierce* in French?"

"No. I never took French. I'll be way behind in French at the Gregory School. I'll have to be in French class with the babies."

"You can call yourself a baby name, then. Like Polly Golly." It seemed a very strange name to

Harriet, but Ole Golly and George had chosen it for their daughter and said that it had *insouciance*.

Harriet smoothed the time line and looked at the place under AGE TWELVE, subcategory THANKSGIVING DAY, where Polly's impending birth had been announced:

POLLY GOLLY WALDENSTEIN DUE IN APRIL.

Ole Golly and George Waldenstein had returned together by train to Montreal on the same day Harriet's parents had finally arrived home.

"You'll come to visit when Polly is born, Harriet," Ole Golly had said, "won't you? And I'll wear my blue silk dress with the embroidered belt. It will fit by then." She laughed and smoothed her tweed things over her swollen middle.

"Maybe I will and maybe I won't," Harriet replied with a sniff. She was sulking a little. She didn't want Ole Golly to leave.

"I humbly beg," Ole Golly said, and Harriet blinked. Ole Golly had never humbly begged before, *ever*.

"Well, all right, I'll come to visit," Harriet told her. "And," she added, "I humbly beg you to hug me goodbye."

"I was going to anyway," Ole Golly told her briskly, and she did.

It was nice, remembering the hug. Harriet wished they had taught her the word for *hug* in French class. "French class is stupid," Harriet told Annie. "They only teach us to talk about food. *Les pommes frites.*"

"I don't mind learning food words. Sport's going to give me cooking lessons," Annie said.

"Sport's in love with you. At least he's in love with Yolanda Montezuma."

"That's the name I used at Sport's school. It's probably one of the reasons I got kicked out. I always call myself Yolanda when I'm feeling aloof."

Harriet thought about *aloof* and decided it was worthy of inclusion on her list of adjectives. "What are you feeling when you're Zoe Carpaccio?" she asked Annie.

Annie thought about it. "Estranged," she said at last, and Harriet decided to add that one to her list too.

"You'll be feeling aloof and estranged at the Gregory School," Harriet warned her, "at least at first. But my advice is: don't act weird."

"No, I'll be okay," Annie said, "because you'll be there, Harriet M. Welsch."

"Except in French class," Harriet reminded her. "And I have to tell you, Annie, I'm feeling a little *sauvage* toward my French teacher. My French teacher never once told me that *enceinte* means pregnant. If I had just known that, I could have saved myself a whole lot of fruitless spying."

"But you *like* spying," Annie pointed out.

"I like *most* parts of it. But I made Sport walk thirty-six blocks on a mission, and it turned out that Ole Golly was simply going to the lab at the hospital for an amnio test to make sure the baby was okay.

"And *also*," Harriet said, beginning to feel a little outraged, "I couldn't figure out why she kept carrying a little bag around, and you know what it was?"

"What?"

"A urine specimen. My mother says they call it *pipi* in French. I am definitely never having a baby if you have to carry *pipi* around."

"Look, I have more stuff than you under AGE TWELVE on my time line," Annie said. "But I've been twelve longer. My birthday was in September. My uncle and aunt took me to a play."

"What do you have under AGE ELEVEN?"

"PARENTS SPLIT AND TURN INTO BASKETS," Annie replied matter-of-factly.

"Excuse me?"

"Basket cases. My parents split up and they turned into basket cases. So I did, too, of course. That's why I act so weird.

"Then below that," Annie went on, "it says GOES TO NEW YORK TO LIVE WITH UNCLE MORRIE AND AUNT BARB."

Harriet gulped. *"Forever?"* she asked.

"No. Just until my parents start acting normal. Like your parents."

Harriet thought about her own parents, stranded in airports, sipping martinis.

She thought about Mr. Waldenstein and Ole Golly, soon to be parents: a roly-poly father who had been deceitful and been forgiven, and a frowny-faced mother who quoted poetry and Dostoievsky and wore tweed things.

Harriet found herself wondering what in the world *normal* meant, after all, and whether it was something that a masterful spy could someday figure out.

She thought for a moment about bad things and good things and how there were always so many of each, and how sometimes they happened in a heap. And then the mixture of things could be rolled up in a rubber band, and it would always be there—in your toy box or your memory or your heart—so you could examine it whenever you wanted, in absolute privacy, wearing your pajamas, or sometimes in the company of an understanding friend.

About the Author

HELEN ERICSON was introduced to Harriet M. Welsch in 1964 when she was nine years old. Ms. Ericson has grown up since then and was elated when the estate of Louise Fitzhugh granted her and Delacorte Press permission to continue Harriet's story in a companion book.

The author lives in a small town in the Midwest with two teenage daughters, a young son, and a large cat named Goldfinger. She has degrees in both religion and law but practices neither. Instead, she is a working journalist who also plays tennis, reads, skis, and sometimes moderates household debates.

Like Harriet M. Welsch, Helen Ericson believes firmly in the importance of muscular verbs and interesting adjectives. *Trounce* and *bestial* are among her favorites.